Winter
in **Lisbon**

Antonio Muñoz Molina

Winter
in Lisbon

Translated from the Spanish
by Sonia Soto

Granta Books
London

Granta Publications, 2/3 Hanover Yard, London N1 8BE

Originally published under the title of *El Invierno en Lisboa*
by Seix Barral, 1987
First published in Great Britain by Granta Books 1999
Copyright © 1987 by Antonio Muñoz Molina
Translation © 1999 by Sonia Soto

Antonio Muñoz Molina has asserted his moral right under the
Copyright, Designs and Patents Act, 1988,
to be identified as the author of this work.

This edition has been translated with the assistance of the
Department for Books, Archives and Libraries
of the Spanish Ministry of Education and Culture.

A CIP catalogue record for this book is available
from the British Library

1 3 5 7 9 10 8 6 4 2

Typeset by M Rules
Printed and bound in Great Britain by
Mackays of Chatham plc

To Andrés Soria Olmedo and Guadalupe Ruiz

To Bill Sherzer, close friend and close reader,
in Spanish and English

'There comes a time in a separation when the loved
one is no longer with you'

Gustave Flaubert, *Sentimental Education*

It was almost two years since I'd last seen Santiago Biralbo, but when I met him again, at midnight, in the Metropolitano, we greeted each other as casually as if we'd been out drinking the night before – not here in Madrid, but back in San Sebastian, at Floro Bloom's bar, where Biralbo used to play.

Now, playing at the Metropolitano, he was joined by a black bass player and a very nervous young French drummer who looked Scandinavian, named Buby. The group called itself the Giacomo Dolphin Trio. I didn't know then that Biralbo had changed his name, that Giacomo Dolphin was not a stage-name for playing the piano but the name which appeared in his passport. Before I saw him, I half recognized his playing. It was as if he put as little effort as possible into the music, as if playing the piano was almost insignificant to him. I'd been sitting at the bar, with my back to the band, when I heard the piano hinting remotely at a song whose name escaped me, and had a sudden feeling of premonition, perhaps that abstract sensation of the past that I've noticed in music sometimes. As I turned I didn't yet realize that what had touched me was a memory of a lost evening at the Lady Bird in San Sebastian, from where there is so much I can't recall. The piano almost disappeared, withdrawing behind the sound of the bass and the drums, and then, looking aimlessly over the faces of the drinkers and the musicians, hazy through the smoke, I saw the profile of Biralbo, playing with his eyes half closed and a cigarette between his lips.

I recognized him immediately, but I can't say he hadn't changed. Perhaps he had, but in an entirely foreseeable way. He wore a dark shirt and black tie, and the passage of time had given his face a concise, upright dignity. Later I realized that I'd always noticed in him that immutable quality of those who live out, unaware, a destiny created for them in adolescence. After thirty, when most of us yield to a decline more ignoble than ageing, they retain a peculiar youthfulness at once fierce and serene, and a quiet, wary courage. The change in Biralbo's face was more noticeable that night, the firm, indifferent or ironic look in his eyes was that of a teenager hardened by experience. I would learn that was why it was difficult to hold his gaze.

For over half an hour I sat drinking cold, dark beer, watching him. He didn't lean over the piano as he played, but held his head up to keep the smoke from his eyes, looking out at the audience, and made quick signals to the other two musicians, his hands moving at a speed that seemed to preclude premeditation or even technique, as if animated by a fate which a second later sounded as notes in the air, organizing themselves in a melody like cigarette smoke forming blue spirals. For whatever reason, this performance seemed to make no claim on Biralbo's attention. I noticed that he glanced frequently at a blonde waitress serving the tables and they once exchanged smiles. He gestured to her and she quickly placed a whisky on top of the piano.

His playing too had changed with the years. I don't listen to music much, and it holds little interest for me, but when I used to hear Biralbo at the Lady Bird I was relieved to find that music could be accessible, could contain stories. That night in the Metropolitano I felt he was even better, but soon I stopped listening to the music and noticed other, smaller differences – how he no longer hunched over the keys, and how sometimes he played with one hand while drinking or resting his cigarette on the ashtray. And I noticed his smile; not the smile he exchanged with the waitress occasionally, but his smiles to the bass player or to himself, with a sudden happiness, oblivious to his surroundings, the way a blind man might smile, certain that no one would guess or share the cause of his joy. Looking at the bass player, I reflected that Biralbo's smile, defiant and proud, was more common in black people. Too much time alone drinking cold beer was making me prone to arbitrary insights: it occurred to me that the Nordic drummer, so lost in himself, was of a different lineage, but between Biralbo and the bassist there was a kind of racial complicity.

After the set they didn't stop to acknowledge the applause. The drummer stood there looking slightly lost, as if dazzled, while Biralbo and the bass player quickly left the stage, chatting in English, laughing with obvious relief, as if a bell had rung ending a long and menial day's work. Greeting a few acquaintances briefly on the way, Biralbo came towards me, although he'd shown no sign of seeing me till then. Maybe before I saw him he had known I was

at the bar, and I suppose he must have studied me as closely as I
had him, and seen more clearly than I could how I'd changed. I
remembered from often seeing him walking alone through the
streets of San Sebastian that he always moved elusively, as if escap-
ing someone. Something of that furtiveness used to show in his
playing. Now, as I watched him head towards me through the
crowd, he seemed slower, more knowing, as if occupying a lasting
area in space. We greeted each other coolly, as always. Ours was an
intermittent, nocturnal friendship, based more on similar tastes in
alcohol – beer, bourbon, white wine, English gin – than on any
unseemly exchange of confidences, to which we were never, or
seldom, given. Self-sufficient drinkers, neither of us trusted the
exaggerations of enthusiasm and affection which came from the
drink and the night; only once, almost at dawn, under the rash
influence of four dry martinis, Biralbo had told me of his love for a
woman I vaguely knew – Lucrecia – and that he'd just returned
from a journey they had made together. We both drank too much
that night. The next day, when I got up, I didn't have a hangover
because I was still drunk, and seemed to have forgotten everything Biralbo had said – I remembered only that their journey,
begun and broken off in haste, was to have ended in Lisbon.

At first we didn't ask many questions or discuss our lives in
Madrid. The blonde waitress approached. Her black and white
uniform smelt faintly of starch, her hair of shampoo. I appreciate
these homely smells in women. Biralbo joked with her and stroked
her hand, and told her to bring him another whisky. I stuck to beer.
After a while San Sebastian was mentioned; and the past, like an
intrusive guest, came and placed itself between us.

'You remember Floro Bloom?' asked Biralbo. 'He had to close
down the Lady Bird. He inherited his father's land and went back

to his village and his childhood sweetheart. I had a letter from him not long ago. He's a farmer and has a son. On Saturday nights he gets drunk at his brother-in-law's bar.'

Compared to the white lights, mirrors, marble tables and smooth walls of the Metropolitano – like an imitation of the dining room in a provincial hotel – the Lady Bird, a basement with brick arches veiled in pinkish gloom, appeared ridiculously anachronistic in my memory, an improbable place for me to have frequented. It was near the sea, and when you emerged on to the street, leaving the music behind, you could hear the waves crashing against the Peine de los Vientos. Then it all came back to me: I could see the phosphorescent foam in the darkness and feel the salt breeze, and I remembered an evening of penitence and dry martinis, ending at the Lady Bird, the last time I had seen Santiago Biralbo.

'But musicians know the past doesn't exist,' he said suddenly, as if dismissing something I'd said. 'Painters and writers accumulate the past on their shoulders, in their words and paintings, but a musician always operates in a void. His music ceases to exist the moment he stops playing. It's pure present.'

'But his records remain.' I wasn't sure I understood what he'd said, or even what I was saying myself, but the beer made me want to disagree.

He looked at me curiously and answered, smiling, 'I made a few records with Billy Swann. Records are nothing. They're dead, or most of them are. And if they're not they're just a way of embalming the present. It's the same with photographs. Eventually they all show a stranger staring out at you. That's why I don't keep any.'

Months later I discovered that he did keep some photographs, but I knew that in fact they confirmed his attitude towards the past, in a perverse, even vindictive way, just as grief or misfortune confirms the will to live, or the way silence, as he would have said, confirms the truth of music.

In fact he did say something like that once in San Sebastian, but in Madrid he no longer seemed so prone to emphatic statements. When he was playing at the Lady Bird, his relationship with music was like a man in love, yielding to a passion stronger than himself, as if to a woman who led him on and rebuffed him and he never understood why happiness was granted or denied. I had often noticed in Biralbo an involuntary inclination towards pathos, in his expression or gestures or in his walk, striking in retrospect because now in the Metropolitano it seemed entirely absent, from both his music and his movements. Now he met your eyes, and no longer looked nervously at doors as they opened. I may have blushed when the blonde waitress realized I was staring at her. I thought: Biralbo's sleeping with her. And I remembered Lucrecia, and the time I met her walking alone along the seafront and she asked me about him. It was drizzling, Lucrecia's damp hair was tied back, and she asked for a cigarette. She seemed reluctantly to have surrendered all pride. We exchanged a few words, then she said goodbye and threw the cigarette away.

'I have rid myself of the blackmail of happiness,' said Biralbo after a brief silence. He was staring at the waitress, who had her back to us. Since our first drink, I'd been waiting for him to mention Lucrecia. But then I realized that, even without actually saying her name, he was talking about her. He went on: 'Happiness and perfection. They're Catholic myths. We get them from the catechism and songs on the radio.'

I said I didn't understand and saw him look at me and smile in the long mirror behind the bar, between rows of gleaming bottles, blurred by cigarette smoke and drowsiness.

'Yes, you do. I'm sure you've woken up some morning and realized you no longer need either happiness or love to make you feel
reasonably alive. It's a relief. As easy as stretching out your hand
and turning off the radio.'

'I suppose you become resigned.' Alarmed at what I'd just said, I
stopped drinking, afraid I might start telling Biralbo my life story.

'You never become resigned,' he said, so quietly that the anger in
his voice was barely perceptible. 'That's another Catholic myth.
You just become wiser, more contemptuous.'

So that was what had happened, what had changed, sharpening
the gleam of courage and knowledge in his cold, haunted eyes. In
two years he had learnt something – maybe only one, terrifying
thing, but it contained his entire life and music. And he'd learnt to
feel contempt and to choose and to play the piano with the irony
and ease of a black man. That was why I no longer knew him. Even
if he hadn't changed his name and gone to live in a hotel, no one,
perhaps not even Lucrecia, would know him now.

It was about two in the morning when we left the bar, silent,
numb, swaying with drink. As I walked with him to his hotel on the
Gran Vía, not far from the Metropolitano, he told me he now
earned his living entirely from performing, though it was irregular
and he led a somewhat nomadic existence, playing clubs in Madrid
mostly, sometimes in Barcelona, and occasionally in Copenhagen
or Berlin, but not as often these days as when Billy Swann was
alive. 'But you can't be pure all the time and live off your music,'
said Biralbo, quoting from the old days. So he sometimes did studio
sessions, for dreadful records on which, luckily, his name didn't
appear. 'It pays well,' he said, 'and once you get out of there you
forget what you played.' If I'd ever heard a piano in one of those
songs on the radio it was probably him. He smiled as he said it, as

if apologizing to himself. But that wasn't so, I thought: he would never again apologize for anything, to anyone. On the Gran Vía, by the cold, gleaming windows of the Telefónica building, he went over to a kiosk to buy cigarettes. As I watched him walk back, tall, swaying, hands sunk in the pockets of his large open overcoat with the collar turned up, I realized that he had that strong air of character one always finds in people who carry a past, as in those who carry a gun. These aren't vague literary comparisons: he did have a past, and he kept a gun.

A couple of days later I bought a Billy Swann record Biralbo had played on. As I've said, I'm pretty much impervious to music. But deep in those songs there was something that touched me, that I almost managed to grasp when I listened to them, but that was always just out of reach. Later, in Biralbo's hotel room among his papers and photographs I found a book which claimed that Billy Swann was one of the greatest trumpet players of the century. On that record it seemed as if he was the only one, as if nobody else in the world had ever played a trumpet, as if he was alone with his voice and his music in the middle of a desert or an abandoned city. On a couple of songs, you could hear his voice, and it was the voice of a ghost, or a dead man. Behind him Biralbo played the piano softly. He appeared as G. Dolphin on the sleeve notes. Two of the songs were his, with the names of places which seemed to me as gentle as the names of women: 'Burma', 'Lisbon'. With the clarity induced by solitary drinking I wondered what it must be like to love a woman called Burma, how her hair and eyes would shine in the darkness. I turned off the record, picked up my raincoat and umbrella, and went to find Biralbo.

The lobby of his hotel was like one of those old cinema foyers reminiscent of a deserted temple. I asked for Biralbo and was told that there was no one of that name there. I described him, gave his room number – 307 – and insisted that he'd been there for a month. The concierge, in a gold-trimmed uniform with a rim of grime round the collar, looked at me with suspicion or conspiracy and said, 'You mean Mr Dolphin.' I nodded, almost guiltily. He called the room but Biralbo wasn't in. A middle-aged bellboy said he'd seen him in the lounge. He added reverently that Mr Dolphin always took his coffee and liqueurs in there.

I found Biralbo reclining on a dubious leather sofa with crude stitching, watching television. Before him were a smoking cigarette and a steaming cup of coffee. He was wearing his coat, as though in a railway station waiting room. The large windows of the lounge looked on to an internal courtyard, and the dingy curtains emphasized the gloom, ushering in the December dusk, as if the night owned the sombre room and was now taking it back. It didn't seem to bother Biralbo and he greeted me with the smile of hospitality which others only use in their dining rooms. There were some poorly executed hunting scenes on the walls and, at the far end, beneath one of those abstract murals that feels like a personal insult, I could make out an upright piano. I found out later that as a guest of long standing Biralbo was granted the modest privilege of practising on it in the mornings. Among the staff there was an exciting suspicion that Mr Dolphin was a famous musician.

He said he liked living in second-rate hotels. With the perverse and steady passion of the solitary man, he loved the beige-carpeted corridors, the closed doors, the succession of room numbers, and the lifts, in which he rarely met another guest. The other residents were anonymous and alone like him, but left their marks — cigarette burns on the floor, scratches or initials in the automatic aluminium door, air stale with unseen people's breath. He returned from work alone when it was almost dawn, or even in full daylight if, as often happened, he allowed the night to prolong itself extravagantly; he told me he enjoyed that strange time in the morning when he seemed to be the only hotel guest around, hearing hoovers humming behind half-closed doors, and always the solitude, the feeling of being dispossessed that elated him as he walked to his room at nine in the morning, turning the key over in his pocket, feeling its weight as if it were the butt of a revolver. In a hotel, he said, nobody deceives you. You don't even have an alibi with which to deceive yourself.

'But Lucrecia wouldn't approve of me living in a hotel like this,' he told me. It was the first time he'd spoken her name. 'She believed in places. Old houses with sideboards and paintings, cafés with mirrors. She'd have loved the Metropolitano. Do you remember the Vienna, in San Sebastian? That was the kind of place she liked to meet her friends. She thought some places were inherently poetic and others weren't.'

As he spoke of Lucrecia he sounded detached, ironic, as people do when constructing a version of their past. I asked about her; he said he didn't know where she was and ordered another coffee. The waiter came and went as though in secrecy, morosely enduring the gift of invisibility. There was an old black and white quiz show on the television. Biralbo glanced at it from time to time with an air of infinite tolerance. He hadn't put on weight but looked bigger or taller, and the coat made him seem larger still.

I visited him in that lounge on many afternoons, and in my memory they all merge into one, long and opaque. I don't know whether it was that first afternoon that he told me to come up to his room. He wanted to give me something for safekeeping.

As we went in he switched on the light, although it wasn't yet dark, and I drew back the curtains to the balcony. Below, across the street, dark-skinned men in anoraks zipped to their necks were starting to congregate at the corner of the Telefónica building while heavily made-up women walked slowly up and down, pausing as if waiting for someone who was late. They seemed mechanical, never getting anywhere and never stopping. Biralbo looked out at the street for a moment and then pulled the curtains closed. The light in the room was dim and gloomy. He took a large suitcase from a wardrobe full of swaying, empty hangers and laid it on the bed. From behind the curtains came the rumble of traffic. Rain started drumming violently very near by, on the awning outside. I could smell winter and the damp of the approaching night, and I thought without nostalgia of San Sebastian, although nostalgia isn't the worst tyranny the distant past can impose. On an evening similar to this one, but very late, almost at dawn, Biralbo and I, exalted or maybe absolved by gin, walked without dignity or umbrellas, bathed by a gentle rain smelling of seaweed and salt, as if touched by compassion – assiduous as a caress, or the familiar streets we walked along. He stopped and raised his face towards the rain, beneath the bare, horizontal branches of the tamarinds, and said, 'I should have been black, played the piano like Thelonius Monk, been born in Memphis, Tennessee. I should be kissing Lucrecia right now, or be dead.'

Now I saw him leaning over the bed, searching among the neatly folded clothes in the suitcase. Suddenly, as I watched his intent face in the wardrobe mirror, it struck me how completely different he was, but I wasn't sure if it made him a better man. The impression lasted only a moment. He soon turned round, holding a packet of letters held together by an elastic band. The envelopes were long, with little blue and red air mail stripes, and bore very small, exotic stamps. They were addressed to Santiago Biralbo in San Sebastian, written in a sloping, feminine hand in violet ink. In the upper left corner, a single initial: *L.* I guessed there were about twenty or twenty-five of them.

Later, Biralbo told me that their correspondence had lasted for two years and then stopped as abruptly as if Lucrecia had died, or never existed. But during that time it was he who felt he didn't exist. As if he were being worn away, he said, by the rubbing of the wind, by his dealings with other people, by absence. He understood then how slowly time passes in closed places, and how tenaciously decay disfigures a painting or turns a stone statue to dust over the centuries. But he only told me these things a month or two after my first visit. Again we were in his room, and he had his revolver close and stood up every few minutes to look out at the street, parting the curtains against which shone the blue light of the sign above the awning. He'd called the Metropolitano to say he was ill. He sat on the bed, smoking, and by the light of the bedside lamp he loaded and cocked the revolver with quick, fluid movements, not talking about the man he expected to see waiting across the street, but about how time passes when nothing is happening, when you're wasting your life waiting for a letter, a telephone call.

'Take this,' he said that first time, looking into my eyes and not at the packet he held out to me. 'Keep these letters somewhere safe, though I probably won't ask for them back.'

He parted the curtains slightly and looked out of the window, tall and calm in his dark coat. In the fading light, with the pavement and cars glistening with rain, an air of neglect hung over the city. I put the letters in my pocket and said I had to leave. Wearily, Biralbo moved away from the window and sat on the bed, feeling his coat pockets and searching the bedside table unsuccessfully for cigarettes. He always smoked short, filterless American cigarettes. I offered him one of mine; he pinched off the filter and lay on the bed. The room was small and I stood awkwardly by the door, unable to repeat that I had to leave. Smoking, his eyes half closed, he probably hadn't heard me the first time. He looked up and gestured towards the only chair in the room. I remembered his song, 'Lisbon': when I heard it, this was exactly how I pictured him, lying in some hotel room, smoking slowly in the translucent gloom. I asked him if he ever got to Lisbon. He laughed, and folded the pillow under his head.

'Of course I did,' he said. 'When the time was right. You get to places when it no longer matters.'

'And you saw Lucrecia there?'

'How do you know?' He sat up, stubbed out the cigarette. I shrugged, more surprised than he was that I'd guessed right.

'I've heard your song, "Lisbon". It reminded me of that trip you began together.'

'That trip,' he repeated. 'That's when I wrote it.'

'But you told me you never got as far as Lisbon.'

'Of course we didn't. That's why I wrote the song. Haven't you ever dreamt that you're lost in a city you've never been to?'

I wanted to ask if Lucrecia had continued the journey alone, but didn't dare. It was obvious he didn't want to talk about it. He glanced at his watch, pretending to be surprised at how late it was, and said the band would be expecting him at the Metropolitano.

He didn't ask me to go along and we parted hurriedly outside the hotel. He set off, turning up his collar, and after a few steps he seemed very far away. When I got home I poured myself a drink and put on the Billy Swann record. When you drink alone you behave like a ghost's valet. You issue orders to yourself and obey them with the vague precision of a servant in a trance: the glass, the ice cubes, the exact measure of gin or whisky, prudently setting down a coaster (heaven forbid you should leave a ring mark on the glass table). I lay on the sofa, resting the wide tumbler on my stomach, and listened to the record for the fourth or fifth time. The tight bundle of letters rested between an ashtray and a bottle of gin. The first song, 'Burma', was full of a darkness and tension sustained to the limit, like fear. Billy Swann's lugubrious voice chanted, 'Burma, Burma, Burma,' as if it was an omen or a psalm, and then the slow, piercing sound of his trumpet stretched on until it shattered into raw notes of chaos and terror. The music was constantly urging me to discover a memory – deserted streets at night, the glare of floodlights on distant street corners, on façades with columns and banks of rubble, figures of men elongated by their shadows, pursuing one another with guns, hats pulled down over their eyes and big overcoats like Biralbo's.

The recollection grew more vivid as I listened, alone, but I knew it wasn't mine; perhaps it came from a film I saw as a child, whose title I'll never know, called up by the persecution and terror in that song. All the things I glimpsed in the music or in myself were contained in a single word, 'Burma', and in the way Billy Swann pronounced it with slow foreboding. *Burma*. Not the name of the country as it appears on a map or in a dictionary, but a hard sound, an incantation. I repeated its two syllables and found there, beneath the drumbeats emphasizing them in the music, words from an ancient language crudely inscribed on stone, or clay tablets, obscure words, indecipherable without sacrilege.

The music stopped. When I got up to put the record back on it was no surprise to feel slightly dizzy and discover that I was drunk. Beside the bottle of gin, the packet of letters lay on the table with the patient, immobile air of lost objects. I removed the rubber band and immediately regretted it, but by then the letters were disordered in my hands. I stared at them, examining the dates of the postmarks, the name of the city – Berlin – where they were posted, the variations in ink colour and handwriting. One of them, the most recent, hadn't been posted. It bore stamps, and Biralbo's address was hurriedly scrawled on it, but there was no postmark. The envelope was much slimmer than the others. Halfway through my next gin I overcame my scruples and looked inside. There was nothing. The last letter Biralbo received from Lucrecia was an empty envelope.

We didn't always meet at the Metropolitano or his hotel. In fact, after he gave me the letters, it was some time before we saw each other again, as though we both felt we'd indulged in an excess of confidences which could only be righted by keeping our distance for a few weeks. I listened to the Billy Swann record and, occasionally, looked at each of the long envelopes in turn, torn open with an impatience which Biralbo would no longer recognize in himself, but I seldom felt tempted to read the letters. There were even days when I forgot all about them lying among a confusion of books and old newspapers. But with a single glance at the neat handwriting and faded violet ink I could easily picture Lucrecia: maybe not the woman Biralbo loved and spent three years waiting for, but the one I sometimes saw around San Sebastian, at Floro Bloom's bar, or on the Paseo Maritimo or Paseo de los Tamarindos, with a deliberate, lost look and an attentive smile which seemed both to ignore you and envelop you for no apparent reason in the warm certainty of her affection, as if you didn't matter to her in the slightest, and were the very person she wanted to see just at that moment. I thought there was a vague similarity between Lucrecia and the city where Biralbo and I had met her, the same extravagant and useless serenity, the same desire to appear both welcoming and alien, that deceptive tenderness in Lucrecia's smile, in the bunches of tamarinds and in the pink sunsets reflected in the slow surf of the bay.

The first time I saw her was at Floro Bloom's bar, maybe the same night Billy Swann and Biralbo played there. I would generally end my evenings at the Lady Bird, sustained by the vague belief that this was where I'd find the improbable women who would agree to go to bed with me when dawn brought on the urgency of desire as the lights of the last bars went out. But that night my purpose was a little more specific. I had an appointment with Bruce Malcolm, sometimes known as the American. He was the correspondent for a couple of foreign art journals, and dealt, I was told, in the illegal export of paintings and antiques. I was always short of money then and a friend who'd been in similar straits said that the American, Malcolm, would buy a couple of rather gloomy religious paintings I owned for a good price, and pay in dollars. I called him. He came round and examined the paintings with a magnifying glass, wiping the darkest areas with cotton wool soaked in something that smelt like alcohol. He spoke Spanish with a South American accent, in a high-pitched, persuasive voice. He conscientiously photographed the paintings, having placed them opposite an open window, and a few days later he rang to say he'd be prepared to pay fifteen hundred dollars for them – seven hundred on delivery, the rest when his partners or bosses in Berlin received them.

We arranged to meet at the Lady Bird. At a secluded table he handed me seven hundred dollars in used notes, having first counted them as slowly as a Victorian cashier. I never saw the other eight hundred, but he'd have been cheating me even if he'd kept his word. I stopped caring about it years ago. More importantly, he wasn't alone when he arrived at the Lady Bird that evening. He was with a tall, very slim girl, who leant forward slightly as she walked and showed very white, slightly separated teeth when she smiled. She had straight, shoulder-length hair, wide, somewhat childlike cheeks, and her nose followed an irregular line. I don't know if I'm remembering her as I saw her that night, or if what I'm picturing as I describe her is one of the photos I found among Biralbo's papers. She and Malcolm stood before me, their backs to the empty stage, and Malcolm held her arm with a proud and proprietorial resolve as he said to me: 'I'd like to introduce you to my wife, Lucrecia.'

When the American finished counting the money we drank to the success of our transaction, as he put it, looking suspiciously pleased with himself. I had the doubly uncomfortable feeling that I was being cheated and that I was taking part in a film without having been given my lines. This often happens to me when I drink with strangers. Malcolm talked and drank a great deal, offering advice on everything from buying paintings to giving up smoking (the key was personal balance, he said, smiling broadly and waving the smoke away from his face as he wrote the name of a brand of nicotine sweets on a napkin). Lucrecia's drink stood untouched in front of her. She seemed able to remain completely herself wherever she was, immune to everything around her, but I

changed my mind when Biralbo started playing. It was just him and
Billy Swann; the absence of the double bass and drums gave the
music, and their lonely presence on the narrow stage of the Lady
Bird, a spare, abstract quality, like a Cubist painting reduced to its
outline. I can remember, even though it was five years ago, that I
hadn't noticed the music start until Lucrecia turned away to face
the far end of the room where the two men were playing,
enveloped in shadows and iridescent smoke. It was a single gesture,
a secret flash as brief as lightning, like a glance caught fleetingly in
a mirror. Emboldened by the whisky and the thought of seven
hundred dollars in my pocket – in those days any large sum of
money seemed infinite, prompting me to indulge in taxis on
impulse and expensive liqueurs – I tried to engage Lucrecia in conversation while the inebriated American looked on benignly. But
the moment the music started, Malcolm and I didn't exist. She
tensed her lips, placed her long hands between her knees and
shook her hair from her face. Malcolm said, 'My wife's a great
music fan,' and refilled my glass. Perhaps this isn't exactly what
happened, maybe when Biralbo started to play Lucrecia didn't look
away from me, but what I do know is that in that instant there was
a change in her that Malcolm and I both noticed. Something happened; not on stage, where Biralbo held his hands over the
keyboard and Billy Swann, still silent, raised his trumpet slowly,
ritually, but between Lucrecia and Malcolm, in the space of the
table where our drinks now stood forgotten, in the silence that I
tried to ignore, like a suddenly unwelcome acquaintance.

The Lady Bird was full of people, all applauding, and a couple of
kneeling photographers dazzled Billy Swann with their flashguns.
Floro Bloom rested his bulk on the bar – fat, blond, jovial, with
small blue eyes, he looked like a Scandinavian woodcutter.

Lucrecia, Malcolm and I tried unsucessfully to listen to the music, the only people not clapping. Billy Swann wiped his forehead with a handkerchief and said something in English, ending with an obscene laugh that provoked more applause, quieter this time. Biralbo translated Swann's words and announced the next song, his mouth very close to the microphone, fatigue audible in his voice. Malcolm was meditatively re-reading the receipt I'd handed him. Through the smoke, Biralbo's eyes met mine, but it wasn't me they were searching for. They fixed on Lucrecia, as if there was nobody in the Lady Bird but her, as if they were alone in an anonymous crowd that watched their every movement. Looking at her, Biralbo said the name of the song they were going to play, first in English, then in Spanish. (Five years later, in Madrid, I felt a shiver of recognition: it was also on the Billy Swann record that I listened to, staring at a handful of letters that had crossed the whole of Europe and the indifference of time to end up in a stranger's hands.) '"All The Things You Are",' said Biralbo, and between his words and the first notes of the song there was a short silence during which nobody dared clap. Malcolm and I both noticed the smile that lit up Lucrecia's eyes without reaching her lips.

I've noticed that foreigners will, without hesitation or warning, switch off their friendliness or their excessive politeness. Under Biralbo's gaze, and with Floro Bloom watching from the bar, Malcolm suddenly announced that he and Lucrecia had to leave, and held out his hand to me. Very serious, and without getting up, she said something to him in English, a few quick words, polite and cold. I saw him pick up his glass, then put it back down on the table, his hard, paint-stained fingers around it as though contemplating breaking it. But he did nothing. While Lucrecia was talking I noticed that Malcolm's head was slightly flattened, like a lizard's.

She wasn't angry: it didn't appear as if she ever could be. She looked at Malcolm as if common sense were enough to disarm him, and the careful way she pronounced each word emphasized the gentleness of her voice, and almost masked her irony. When Malcolm spoke again he did so in atrocious Spanish. Fury distorted his pronunciation, turning him back into a stranger in a country and a language in league against him. Ignoring me and looking only at Lucrecia, he said: 'You know why you wanted us to come here.' My presence meant nothing to either of them.

I decided to take an interest in my cigarettes and the music. Malcolm backed down. Taking a wad of notes from his trouser pocket he went over to the bar. He stood talking to Floro Bloom for a moment, waving the money a little smugly, or perhaps angrily. Out of the corner of his eye he watched Lucrecia sitting at the table, and Biralbo, lost in his own world at the piano, very far from us. Occasionally Biralbo raised his eyes, and Lucrecia straightened minutely, as though trying to see him over a wall. Malcolm slammed the money down on the counter and disappeared into the darkness at the back of the bar. Lucrecia stood up, blotting me out with a smile, dismissing me just as one waves aside cigarette smoke, and walked over to Floro Bloom. The sound of Billy Swann's trumpet sliced through the air like a knife. Lucrecia gestured in front of Floro Bloom's drowsy face and she soon held a piece of paper and a pen. She wrote something quickly, while eyeing both the stage and the red-lit corridor down which Malcolm had disappeared. She folded the paper, leant over to hide it behind the bar, and gave the pen back to Floro. By the time Malcolm reappeared, barely a minute later, Lucrecia was telling me how to get to their flat and inviting me to dinner, any time I wanted. She lied with calm and conviction, almost with tenderness.

Neither of them shook my hand as they left. The curtain of the Lady Bird closed behind them and it was as if the applause that started at that moment was meant for them. It was the only time I saw them together. I never received the eight hundred dollars for my pictures and I never saw Malcolm again. Nor, in a way, did I ever see that Lucrecia again: the one I saw later was different, paler, with much longer hair. She was less serene, her will crushed – grave and intense, as if she had glimpsed true darkness and been sullied by it. Fifteen days after that meeting at the Lady Bird, she and Malcolm left on a cargo ship bound for Hamburg. Their landlady said they owed three months' rent. Only Santiago Biralbo knew they were going, but he wasn't at the port to see them secretly board the fishing boat at midnight. Lucrecia had told him that the freighter was waiting out at sea, and she didn't want him to come to the port to see her off from a distance. She said she'd write, and she gave him a card with an address in Berlin. Biralbo put it in his pocket and headed quickly back to the Lady Bird. Perhaps he was thinking of another piece of paper and another message – waiting for him one night two weeks before – when he finished playing with Billy Swann and went to the bar to ask Floro for a glass of gin or bourbon.

Waking late on Sundays in Madrid I'd have beer for breakfast because I found it slightly embarrassing asking for a white coffee in a bar at midday. On those winter Sunday mornings in certain parts of the city there's a cold, calm light that intensifies the transparency of the air, a brightness that sharpens the edges of the white buildings and makes footsteps and voices echo as though the city was deserted. I liked reading the paper in a clean, empty bar, drinking just enough beer to see me through till lunch in a state of optimistic indolence, looking at everything as if peering, notebook in hand, into a glass-walled honeycomb. Around two-thirty I carefully folded my newspaper and threw it away, and the sense of weightlessness made my walk to the restaurant very peaceful. It was an old, well-kept establishment, with a zinc-topped bar and cubic glass flasks of wine, where the waiters knew me but didn't behave with the irritating familiarity that often made me flee from similar places.

One of those Sundays, while I was waiting for my meal at a back table, Biralbo arrived with a very attractive woman. After a moment I recognized the blonde waitress from the Metropolitano. They had the relaxed and smiling air of a couple who had just woken up together, and went to stand with the other people waiting at the bar. I watched them for a while, wondering whether to call to them. I decided I didn't mind that the waitress's hair was dyed blond. She wore a short skirt and slate-grey tights. As they talked, cigarettes and beer glasses in hand, Biralbo lightly stroked her back and waist. She hadn't done her hair but had put on a pink, almost mauve, lipstick. I pictured cigarette ends stained that colour lying in an ashtray on a bedside table, and reflected, sad and somewhat bitter, that I'd never been granted a woman like her. I stood up and called out to Biralbo.

The blonde waitress – Monica – ate quickly and left, saying she had an afternoon shift at the Metropolitano. On her way out she made me promise we'd meet again and kissed me very close to the mouth. Biralbo and I remained alone, looking at each other warily over our coffee and cigarette smoke, each knowing what the other was thinking, avoiding the words that would take us back to our only possible point of departure, the endless succession of futile evenings that all merged into just one or two. When we were alone, even without saying anything, it was as if there had been nothing else in our lives but those nights long ago at the Lady Bird in San Sebastian. Knowing what we shared, clinging to a past that was scorned or lost, we were condemned to oblique conversations, or cautious silence.

The restaurant was almost empty, the metal shutters already

half lowered. Out of the blue I mentioned Malcolm. It was a way of referring to Lucrecia, a prelude allowing us to remember her without mentioning her name. With heavy irony I related the story of the paintings and the eight hundred dollars I never received. He glanced round as if to make sure Monica had gone and burst out laughing.

'So old Malcolm cheated you too.'

'He didn't cheat me. I knew at the time he wasn't going to pay.'

'But you didn't care. Deep down it made no difference to you. But it did to him. I'm pretty sure he paid for his journey to Berlin with that money. They wanted to leave but couldn't. Suddenly Malcolm came back and said he'd bribed the captain of that cargo ship to let them travel in the hold. You paid for their passage.'

'Is that what Lucrecia told you?'

Biralbo laughed again, as if at himself this time, and then drank some coffee. No, Lucrecia hadn't told him anything, not even that they were leaving until the very last day. They never talked about real things, as though keeping silent about their separate lives protected them more than the lies she told to see him, or the locked doors of the hotel rooms where they met for half an hour when there wasn't time to go to Biralbo's flat. The future dissolved with their first embrace. She would look at her watch, and get dressed, concealing the pink marks on her neck with face powder that Biralbo had bought one day on her instructions, eyed suspiciously by the shop assistant. He couldn't bear to say goodbye at the lift so he went down with her and watched as she drove off in a taxi, waving to him.

Sometimes he thought of Malcolm, alone, waiting, ready to search for the scent of another's body on her clothes or in her hair. He would go back to his flat or hotel room and lie on the bed, tormented by envy and loneliness, or wander about, trying to hurry time, to fill the empty hours or even entire days before he could be with Lucrecia again. All he saw was clocks with hands that seemed stuck, and something dark and profound like a tumour, a shadow that no light could dispel – the life she was living at that very moment, with Malcolm, in Malcolm's flat, where Biralbo once secretly went, to create a memory, not of a moment of tenderness stolen there with Lucrecia (they were terrified Malcolm might return early from his trip, and every sound was his key turning in the lock) but of her other life, which was afterwards as vivid in Biralbo's mind as only real things can be. His pain might have been less intense had he never been to the flat and didn't now have such a precise memory of it. Malcolm's shaving brush and razor on a glass shelf, beneath the mirror in the bathroom, his dressing gown, of a flimsy blue fabric, hanging behind the bedroom door, his felt slippers under the bed, a photograph of him on the bedside table next to the alarm clock that woke them both every morning . . . The unmistakable smell of Malcolm's cologne in every room, on his towels, a faint reminder of her intimacy with another man, repelling the usurper. Malcolm's untidy studio, with pots full of paintbrushes and bottles of turpentine and reproductions of paintings tacked roughly to the wall.

Biralbo had been leaning back in his chair as he described this, smiling and dropping ash into his coffee cup, but suddenly he sat up and looked at me sharply. Something had just come back to him, like those objects we sometimes find out of place and which make us truly look at what we have ceased to see.

'I saw those paintings you sold him,' he said. He was astonished to be seeing them clearly again, and afraid of losing the image. 'In one of them there was a sort of allegorical figure, a blindfolded woman holding something . . .'

'A glass. A glass and a cross.'

'She had long black hair, and a very pale, round face, with rouged cheeks.'

I would have liked to ask if he knew where the pictures ended up, but by then he didn't care much about what I might say. He was seeing something with a clarity his memory had denied him until then, a stratum of time in its pure state; the image of a painting he'd never tried to remember was now bringing back to him intact a few hours of his past with Lucrecia and, like a beam of light trained on a single face which expands to illuminate an entire room, he gradually remembered the things surrounding the painting that afternoon – Lucrecia standing close to him, their fear of Malcolm returning, the oppressive, late September light in all the rooms they entered, not knowing that these would be their last real minutes together for three years.

'Malcolm spied on us,' said Biralbo. 'On me. I saw him near my flat several times, lurking like some stupid detective – you know, standing on the corner with a newspaper, or having a drink in the bar opposite. Those foreigners believe in films too much. Sometimes he came to the Lady Bird on his own and sat at the far end of the bar, pretending to listen to the music or Floro Bloom, but really he was watching me. I didn't care, it was even a little amusing, but one evening Floro said to me very seriously: "Be careful, that guy's got a gun."'

'Did Malcolm ever threaten you?'

'He threatened Lucrecia, ambiguously. His business was sometimes pretty risky. They wouldn't have left as quickly as they did if

Malcolm hadn't been scared of something. He had dealings with
dangerous people and wasn't as brave as he looked. Soon after he
bought your pictures he went to Paris for a couple of days. That's
when I went to his flat. When he got back he told Lucrecia there
were lots of people who wanted to cheat him, and he took out a
gun and put it on the table while they were having supper. He pretended to clean it. He said he had a whole clip of bullets ready for
anyone who tried to cheat him.'

'Empty threats,' I said. 'From a deceived husband.'

'He'd told Lucrecia he was going to Paris to see some Cézannes
in a museum, but I'd swear he never went. He lied so he could spy
on us. I'm sure he saw us go to the flat and waited near by. Maybe
he wanted to come up and catch us but didn't dare.'

As Biralbo said this I shuddered. We were finishing our coffee.
The waiters had already laid the tables for dinner and were looking at us with undisguised impatience. It was five in the
afternoon and I could hear a heated discussion about a football
match on the radio, but suddenly I saw an ordinary street in San
Sebastian, from above, as in a film, a man standing on the pavement, looking up at a window, gripping a gun in his pocket and
a newspaper under his arm, stamping to thaw his frozen feet.
Later, I realized that this was what Biralbo feared when he
looked out of his hotel window in Madrid. A man waiting and
trying to look inconspicuous, but not too hard, just enough for
whoever was meant to see him to know he was there and wasn't
going to go away.

We stood up and Biralbo paid. He refused my money, saying he
wasn't a poor musician any more. Outside, the sun still caught the
tops of buildings, the windows and the tower that looks like a lighthouse on the Hotel Victoria. But there was an opaque, coppery

quality to the light at the ends of the streets and an evening chill
hung in all the doorways. I felt the old anxiety that always took
hold of me on winter Sunday afternoons, so I was relieved when
Biralbo suggested we go to a bar he knew – not the Metropolitano,
but an empty, anonymous place. Company couldn't alleviate my
despair on afternoons like this, with the gleam of headlights on
asphalt and neon signs against a night sky still tinged with red in the
distance, but it was better to be with someone than return home,
walking back alone along the wide Madrid streets.

'They left in a terrible hurry, as if someone was after them,' said
Biralbo after a few bars and futile gins, as though there had been no
break in the conversation. 'They'd been thinking of settling permanently in San Sebastian. Malcolm wanted to open an art gallery,
and was even about to rent a place. But when he got back from
Paris, or wherever he went for those two days, he told Lucrecia
they had to go to Berlin.'

'What he wanted was to get her away from you,' I said; alcohol
gave me flashes of lucidity about other people's lives.

Biralbo smiled and looked intently at the level of gin in his
glass. Before answering he reduced it by a good half inch.

'There was a time when it flattered me to think so, but I'm no
longer sure. I think, deep down, he didn't care if Lucrecia slept with
me from time to time.'

'You don't know how he was looking at you that night at the
Lady Bird. Don't you remember those staring blue eyes?'

'It didn't bother him because he knew Lucrecia was his and
nobody else's. She could have stayed with me, but she left with
him.'

'She was scared of him. I saw what he was like that night. You
told me he threatened her with a gun.'

'A nine-millimetre. But she wanted to leave, and just took the opportunity Malcolm offered her. A fishing boat or a smugglers' ship, a Hamburg-registered freighter – I think it had a woman's name, Berta or Lotte or something. Lucrecia had read too many books.'

'She was in love with you. I saw it. Anyone who saw her that night would have noticed, even Floro Bloom. She left you a note, didn't she? I saw her write it.'

Absurdly, I was intent on proving to Biralbo that Lucrecia loved him. Indifferent, vaguely grateful, he went on drinking and let me talk. He blew out smoke, his hand covering his mouth and chin, holding the cigarette to his lips; I could never read what was behind the intense gleam in his eyes. Perhaps he was remembering not grief or hard words but the trivial things that had, unnoticed, made up the interweaving strands of his life, the note, for instance, with the time and place for them to meet. He kept it for a long time, until it seemed like a remnant of someone else's life, like the letters he entrusted to me which I haven't read, and never will. He started to fidget, glancing impatiently at his watch, and said he was due at the Metropolitano soon. I thought of the blonde waitress, with her slim legs, her smile and perfume. But I stubbornly continued to ask questions. I pictured Malcolm's face at the Lady Bird and it became the face of the man waiting, pacing slowly beneath a window, stopping occasionally in the light San Sebastian rain. Biralbo was at Malcolm's flat, where Lucrecia had arranged to meet him; maybe it was she who had suggested to Malcolm that he arrange to pay me at the Lady Bird two days before . . . Malcolm kept watch over her all the time, so how else could she leave Biralbo a note? I realized my thoughts were going round in circles. If Malcolm was so suspicious, if he noticed even the slightest change in Lucrecia's eyes and was sure that as soon as he stopped watching her she would go to meet Biralbo, then why didn't he take her with him to Paris?

The note read: *Thursday at seven at my place phone first don't speak until you hear my voice.* And at the bottom, as in the letters, a single initial: L. She wrote it so fast she left out the commas, Biralbo said, but the handwriting was still as perfect as a display of calligraphy. A sloping hand, meticulously neat, almost solicitous, like a sign of politeness, like Lucrecia's smile when Malcolm introduced us. Maybe she smiled at him like that when she went to see him off at the station, then walked away, got into a taxi and arrived home just in time to greet Biralbo. The same smile, I thought, and immediately felt guilty: that thought should have occurred to Biralbo not me.

'Did she actually see him leave?' I asked. 'Are you sure she waited until the train set off?'

'How should I know? I suppose she did, with him leaning out of the window to say goodbye, that kind of thing. But he could have got off at the next station, on the border at Irún.'

'When did he get back?'

'Two days later, maybe three. But I didn't hear from Lucrecia for almost two weeks. I got Floro Bloom to ring her at home, but there was no answer, and she didn't leave me any more messages at the Lady Bird. One evening I summoned the courage to ring her myself. Somebody picked up the phone and put it down without saying anything – I couldn't tell if it was Malcolm or her. I walked up and down her street and watched her door from the café opposite, but I never saw them come out. I couldn't even see if they were there in the evenings because the shutters were closed.'

'I called Malcolm too, to ask for my eight hundred dollars.'

'And did you get to speak to him?'

'No, never. Were they hiding?'

'I expect Malcolm was organizing his getaway.'

'Didn't Lucrecia ever explain?'

'All she said was that they were leaving. She didn't have time to say much more. I was at the Lady Bird early one evening, just before it opened. I was practising at the piano and Floro Bloom was laying the tables when the telephone rang. I stopped playing; at each ring my heart missed a beat. I was sure it was Lucrecia this time and was terrified the phone would stop ringing. Floro took ages to answer – you remember how slowly he moved. When he got to it I was standing in the middle of the bar, not daring to go any nearer. Floro said something and looked at me. He shook his head a lot and said yes several times, then hung up. I asked who it was. "Who do you think?" he said. "Lucrecia. She'll be waiting for you in fifteen minutes under the colonnade in the Plaza de la Constitución."'

It was an evening at the beginning of October, when night falls early and catches you by surprise when you leave the house, as if you've woken up on a train which has taken you to another country where it's already winter. When Biralbo had arrived at the Lady Bird it was still early, with a warm, yellow light in the air, but by the time he left it was dark, and rain lashed the cliffs as viciously as the waves. He ran in search of a taxi, because the Lady Bird was almost at the end of the bay, some distance from the centre of town. By the time a taxi stopped he was soaked and almost unable to tell the driver where he wanted to go. He peered through the darkness at the illuminated clock on the dashboard, but didn't know exactly when he'd left the Lady Bird, feeling lost in time, that he'd never get to the Plaza de la Constitución. And even if he did arrive, even if the taxi found its way through the chaos of streets and cars, out there behind the curtain of rain that closed again almost as soon as the windscreen wipers parted it, Lucrecia would probably have left, five minutes or maybe five hours before – he no longer had any sense of time passing.

He couldn't see her when he got out of the taxi. The corner streetlamps weren't strong enough to light up the gloomy, damp interior of the colonnade. He listened to the taxi drive away and stood still while all his feelings of urgency turned to shock. For a moment he couldn't remember what he was doing in that dark, deserted square.

'And then I saw her,' said Biralbo. 'I didn't feel any more surprised than if I shut my eyes now and opened them to see you. She was leaning against the wall, by the library steps, almost completely in the darkness, but from a distance I could see her white shirt. It was a summer shirt, under a dark blue three-quarter length coat. From the way she smiled I realized we weren't going to kiss. She said, "Look at the rain." I said that it rains like that in films when people are going to say goodbye.'

'Is that how you talked to each other?' I asked, but Biralbo didn't seem to understand why I was surprised. 'You hadn't seen each other for two weeks and that's all you had to say?'

'Her hair was wet, like mine, but her eyes were dull. She was carrying a big plastic bag – she'd told Malcolm she was going to pick up a dress, so she could only stay a few minutes. She asked me how I knew this meeting was our last. "From the movies," I said. "The rain always means someone's leaving for good."'

Lucrecia had glanced at her watch – the gesture Biralbo most dreaded – and said she had ten minutes to go for a coffee. They went to the only bar under the colonnade that was open, a dirty place reeking of fried fish that bothered Biralbo more than Lucrecia's distance, or the way time was vanishing. Sometimes you take a fraction of a second to accept the sudden loss of all that has been yours: just as light is faster than sound, conscious- ness is quicker than grief, and dazzles you like a silent flash of lightning. So Biralbo felt nothing as he looked at Lucrecia that evening and didn't fully appreciate the meaning of her words or the look on her face. Real pain came only several hours later. And then he tried to remember their exact words, but couldn't. He understood that absence was a neutral sensation of emptiness.

'She didn't say why they were leaving like that? On a cargo ship run by smugglers, and not by plane, or train?'

Biralbo shrugged: no, that kind of question hadn't occurred to him. He asked her to stay, knowing what her answer would be. He asked just once, he didn't plead. 'Malcolm would kill me,' Lucrecia said. 'You know what he's like. He brought out his German gun again yesterday.' But there was no fear in her voice, as though the possibility that Malcolm might kill her was no more worrying than being late for an appointment. 'Lucrecia was like that,' said Biralbo, with the serenity of one who's finally understood something. Any sign of fervour in her had disappeared and she looked as if she didn't care if she lost everything she'd ever had or wanted. 'As if she'd never cared,' Biralbo added.

She didn't touch her coffee. They both stood, separated by the table, by the noise of the bar, already living in that future where distance would confine each of them. Lucrecia looked at her watch and smiled before saying she had to go. For a moment her smile was the same as a fortnight before, when they parted before dawn, beside a door bearing Malcolm's name on a brass plate. Biralbo stood watching Lucrecia disappear into the gloom under the colonnade. She'd left him one of Malcolm's cards with an address in Berlin written in pencil on the back.

That song, 'Lisbon'. When I listened to it I was back in San Sebastian, the way you're transported back to places in dreams. A city is forgotten more quickly than a face; remorse or emptiness replaces the memory, and, as with a face, the city remains intact only where your mind has failed to erode it. You dream about it, but don't always deserve the memory of the dream, and in any case it's lost after a few hours, or even minutes, as you lean over to splash your face with cold water or drink your coffee. Santiago Biralbo seemed immune to this ailment. He said he never thought about San Sebastian; he wanted to be like a film hero whose life story begins with the plot and has no past, only imperious qualities. The Sunday night he told me about Lucrecia and Malcolm's departure he said, as we parted at the Metropolitano, where we'd arrived late and very drunk: 'Pretend we met each other here for the first time. You weren't seeing someone you already knew, just a man who played the piano.' He indicated a poster for his band and added: 'Remember, I'm Giacomo Dolphin now.'

But his claim that music was free of the past was a lie; 'Lisbon' was a pure experience of time, intact and transparent, as if sealed in a glass bottle. It was both Lisbon and San Sebastian, in the same way that someone in a dream can be two people at once. At first it sounded like the needle tracking at the start of a record, which became the sound of brushing on cymbals and a beat like a heart close by. Only then did the trumpet trace a cautious melody. Billy Swann played as though afraid of waking someone. A minute later Biralbo came in, leading you hesitantly along a path and then seeming to disappear in darkness, only to reappear when the music was at its fullest, revealing the entire form of the melody, as if while lost in a mist you were lifted to the top of a hill from where you could see a town spread out below, bathed in light.

I've never been to Lisbon, and it's years since I was in San Sebastian. I remember ochre façades darkened by rain, stone balconies, an esplanade tight against a wooded hillside, and an avenue imitating a Parisian boulevard, lined with tamarinds, their branches bare in winter, but hung in May with strange bouquets of pale pink flowers reminiscent of the foam on waves in the summer dusk. I remember abandoned *quintas* overlooking the sea, the island and the lighthouse in the middle of the bay whose curve of lights twinkled like undersea stars. In the distance, at the far end of the bay, was the pink and blue neon sign of the Lady Bird, the sailing boats at anchor named after women or countries, and fishing boats smelling powerfully of damp wood, petrol and seaweed.

Malcolm and Lucrecia boarded one of these boats, perhaps afraid of losing their balance as they carried their suitcases across the unsteady, creaking gangway – heavy suitcases, filled with old paintings and books, and all the things you can't bear to abandon when you've decided to leave a place for good. Listening with relief to the slow rumble of the motor as the boat headed out into the dark, they must have turned to see the lighthouse far away on the island, the lights of the town against the night sky one last time, sinking slowly across the expanse of sea. At that hour Biralbo would have been sitting at the bar of the Lady Bird, drinking straight bourbon, accepting Floro Bloom's melancholy companionship. I wondered if Lucrecia managed to make out the distant lights of the Lady Bird, or if she even tried.

She must have looked for them when she returned to the city three years later, relieved to see them still there, without wanting to go in. She disliked visiting places where she'd once lived, and meeting old friends, even Floro Bloom, her placid accomplice in alibis and assignations, her motionless messenger.

Biralbo had given up believing she would return. He had changed his life in those three years. He got fed up with the humiliation of playing the electric organ at the Vienna Café and vulgar parties out in the suburbs, so he took a job teaching music in a Catholic girls' school. But he still played at the Lady Bird a couple of nights a week, even though Floro Bloom, resigned to being driven out of business by the disloyalty of his nocturnal clientele, could barely afford to pay for his drinks. Biralbo got up at eight and spent the day explaining music theory and talking about Liszt and Chopin and the Clair de Lune sonata in indistinguishable classrooms full of teenage girls in blue uniforms. He lived alone in a block of flats on the river, far from the sea. He travelled into town on a suburban train nicknamed the Mole, and waited for letters from Lucrecia. At that time we hardly ever saw each other. I heard he'd given up performing, that he was going to leave San Sebastian, that he'd given up drinking, or become an alcoholic, that Billy Swann had called and asked him to play with him in Copenhagen. I bumped into him a couple of times. I saw him one morning on his way to work, looking docile and absent-minded, his hair still damp and hurriedly combed back, wearing a tie and carrying a sober briefcase full of unmarked exam papers. He looked like someone who had recently given up a dissolute life. He walked very fast staring at the ground, as if late, or fleeing without conviction from a mediocre awakening. Then one evening I came across him in a bar in the old town, on the Plaza de la Constitución. He bought me a drink. He was already a little drunk and said he was celebrating his thirty-first birthday, and that after a certain age you had to celebrate your birthday alone. Around midnight he paid and stood up to leave abruptly – he had to rise early the next day, he explained, hunching over as he turned up his coat collar, thrust his hands into his pockets and secured his briefcase under his arm. In those days there was something strangely final about his departures: as soon as he said goodbye he was utterly alone.

He wrote letters and waited for replies, gradually constructing an entirely secret existence in which neither time nor reality intervened. At five every afternoon, after he finished teaching, he caught the train home, tie straight and briefcase under his arm, looking like a tax inspector. He read a newspaper during the brief journey, or stared at the tall blocks of flats and small villages dotted about the hills. At home he locked the door and played records. He had an upright piano, bought in instalments, but rarely played

it, preferring to listen to music, lying flat on his back and smoking.
Never again would he hear so many records or write so many letters. At the entrance to his block of flats, even before taking out
the key, he peered into his box to see whether there was a letter,
trembling as he unlocked it. For the first two years, he received a
letter from Lucrecia every two or three weeks but still hoped to
find one every afternoon, living for it from the moment he woke
up, but most days there were just bank statements, letters from the
school and fliers that he threw away, angry and slightly bitter. Any
envelope with airmail stripes filled him with joy.

But two years after she left, the letters stopped, and he couldn't
say he hadn't been expecting it. For six months not a day passed
when he didn't hope for a final letter from Lucrecia, and then it
arrived. But not by post: Billy Swann brought it, months after it was
written.

I still remember Billy Swann's return to San Sebastian. There are
some cities where everything finishes, and others to which you
always return; San Sebastian is one of these, even though you
feel at the very end of the earth when staring out at the estuary
from the last bridge on winter evenings, watching the water
recede and the white waves that look like horses' manes, galloping
out of the darkness. The Kursaal Bridge, which sounds like it
could span a river in South Africa, has tall yellow beacons at either
end that resemble lighthouses on a dangerous coast, forewarnings
of a shipwreck. But I know that it's a city you go back to and
some day I'll prove it; any other city – Madrid – is just a place to
pass through.

Billy Swann returned from America, apparently barely avoiding
charges of drug possession. Or perhaps he was trying to escape his
slowly declining fame. He had passed into legend and oblivion

almost simultaneously; according to Biralbo very few people who listened to Billy Swann's old records knew he was still alive. In the persistent gloom and emptiness of the Lady Bird he gave Floro Bloom a long hug and asked after Biralbo, taking a moment to remember that Floro didn't understand English. He'd arrived with nothing more than a battered suitcase and his black leather false-bottomed trumpet case. He strode between the empty tables of the Lady Bird and climbing energetically on to the stage removed the piano cover and delicately, almost modestly, played the opening bars of a blues piece. In a Spanish that required of the listener powers of divination rather than attention, he asked Floro Bloom to telephone Biralbo. He had just come out of hospital in New York and now lived in a permanent state of urgency: he was in a hurry to prove he wasn't dead, which was why he'd come back to Europe so quickly. 'Here, a musician's still somebody,' he said to Biralbo, 'but in America they treat you like a dog. In the two months I spent in New York only the Narcotics Bureau paid me any attention.'

He'd come back to Europe to settle permanently and had grandiose, nebulous plans which included Biralbo. He asked Biralbo about his life: he hadn't heard from him in years. Biralbo told me that when he said he was a music teacher in a convent school and almost never played nowadays, Billy Swann was incensed. A bottle of whisky in front of him, his elbows planted firmly on the bar of the Lady Bird, he disowned Biralbo with that holy rage to which old alcoholics are sometimes moved. It reminded Biralbo of the old days, when he was twenty-three or -four and Billy Swann found him playing for beer and sandwiches in a club in Copenhagen. Biralbo wanted to learn everything in those days. He swore he'd be a musician for life and he'd happily go hungry if that was what it took.

'Look at me,' Biralbo told me Swann said. 'I've always been one of the best trumpet players. I was before all those clever guys who write books knew it, and I still am even though they've stopped. But if I died tomorrow you wouldn't find enough money in my pockets to pay for my funeral. But I'm Billy Swann, and when I do die there'll be no one left who can play this trumpet the way I do.'

When he leant his elbows on the bar his sleeves rode up exposing thin, hard wrists snaked with veins. Biralbo noticed how dirty the cuffs were but, with relief bordering on gratitude, saw the showy gold cufflinks he'd so often seen glinting in the stage lights when Billy Swann raised his trumpet. But he feared Billy Swann's words, and his eyes shining and wet behind his lenses; he believed he no longer deserved Billy Swann's approval. He felt guilty and false when he realized how much he'd changed and surrendered during the last few years. Like a stone cast into a deep well, Billy Swann's return shook the stagnation of time. Behind the bar, not understanding a single word, Floro Bloom nodded placidly and made sure their glasses were never empty for long. But maybe he understood everything, Biralbo thought, noticing the look in his blue eyes. Floro Bloom had caught him sneaking a glance at his watch, calculating how little time was left before he had to go to work. Lost in thought, Billy Swann emptied his glass, clicked his tongue and wiped his mouth with a grubby handkerchief.

'I have nothing more to say to you,' he said gravely. 'Now look at your watch again and tell me you have to go home to bed and I'll punch you in the face.'

Biralbo stayed. At nine the next morning he called the school to say he was ill. In Floro Bloom's silent company, they went on drinking for two days. On the third, Billy Swann had to be taken to a clinic and spent a week recovering. He returned to his hotel

looking shaky but dignified, like someone who has just spent a
few days in prison, his hands a little bonier and his speech slightly
less intelligible than before. When Biralbo went to Billy Swann's
room and saw him lying on the bed, he was shocked that he
hadn't noticed before how much his face looked like a dead man's.

'I'm leaving for Stockholm tomorrow,' said Billy Swann. 'I've got
a good contract there. I'll call you in a couple of months. You can
play with me and we'll make a record.'

Hearing this Biralbo felt no joy, or even gratitude, simply fear
and a sense of unreality. If he went to Stockholm he'd lose his job
at the school, and a letter from Lucrecia might arrive and lie use-
lessly in his letterbox for months. I can picture clearly Biralbo's face
during those days: I saw it in a photograph beside a newspaper article reporting Billy Swann's arrival in San Sebastian. It showed a tall,
very old-looking man, his angular face half hidden beneath the
kind of hat supporting actors wore in old films. Beside him, shorter,
disconcerted and looking very young, stood Santiago Biralbo,
although his name didn't appear in the article. That was how I
found out Billy Swann was back. In Madrid, I discovered that
Biralbo had kept the cutting, by then yellowing and blurred, with
his papers, together with a photo in which Lucrecia looked nothing like I remembered, with very short hair and a tense smile.

'I was in Berlin in January,' said Billy Swann. 'I saw your girl
there.'

He hesitated before continuing. Biralbo didn't dare ask anything. He reimmersed himself in the memory that Billy Swann's
return had stirred up: an evening at the Lady Bird, when he'd come
on stage searching for Lucrecia's face among the dark heads of the
audience. He saw her at the back, indistinct in the smoke and pink
lighting, looking firm and serene, sitting at a table with Malcolm

and another man. The man seemed familiar but it had taken him a moment to recognize me.

'I'd been playing at the Satchmo for a couple of nights – a really strange place, like a hookers' bar,' Billy Swann went on. 'She was waiting for me in my dressing room. She took a letter out of her bag and asked me to give it to you. She seemed very nervous, and left straight away.'

Biralbo still said nothing. He couldn't quite believe that after so long someone was speaking to him about Lucrecia, that Billy Swann had actually seen her in Berlin; he felt stunned and slightly afraid. He didn't ask Billy Swann what had happened to the letter, nor did it occur to him to ask why Lucrecia hadn't posted it. He'd heard that Billy Swann had left Berlin three or four months earlier for America, and almost been given up for dead in a New York hospital where he took weeks to regain consciousness. Biralbo didn't want to ask anything because he feared Billy Swann would say, 'I left the letter in my hotel room in Berlin,' or 'My luggage was lost at the airport with the letter inside.' He wanted to read the letter so badly that at that moment he would almost have preferred seeing it to its sender.

'I haven't lost it,' said Billy Swann. He got up and opened his trumpet case, on the bedside table. His hands shook so badly he dropped the trumpet on the floor. Biralbo bent down to retrieve it and by the time he stood up Billy Swann had opened the case's false bottom and was holding out the letter.

Biralbo looked at the stamps, the address, his name written in handwriting that remained unaffected by misfortune or loneliness. For the first time she'd written not simply her initial but her whole name on the envelope: *Lucrecia*. He felt the envelope and it seemed terribly slim, but he couldn't bring himself to open it. It felt smooth

and sensitive to the touch, like the ivory keys of the piano before
he played a note. Billy Swann lay back on the bed. It was an
evening towards the end of May, but he wore a black suit and
heavy shoes, like a corpse. He pulled the bedcover up to his neck
because he'd felt a chill when he got up. His voice was slower and
more nasal than ever, and he sounded as if he was repeating the
opening verses of a blues song over and over.

'I saw your girl. She was sitting there when I opened the door to
my dressing room. It was very small and she was smoking. She
filled the place with smoke.'

'Lucrecia doesn't smoke,' said Biralbo. It gave him a small satisfaction to say it. He knew it as clearly as if he'd suddenly
remembered the colour of her eyes or the way she smiled.

'Well she was smoking when I went in.' Billy Swann was angry
with Biralbo for doubting his memory. 'Before I saw her the smell
of cigarette smoke hit me. I know the difference between that and
marijuana.'

'Do you remember what she said?' Biralbo now dared to ask.
Billy Swann turned very slowly towards him, his monkeyish head
poking out over the white bedcover, and the lines on his face
deepened as he laughed.

'She didn't say much. She thought I might not remember her.
Like those guys I meet from time to time who say to me, "Billy,
don't you remember me? We played together in Boston in fifty-
four." That's the kind of thing she said, but I did remember her
when I saw her legs. I can pick one woman out of twenty just by
looking at her legs. In those badly lit venues you can't see women's
faces past the first row, but you can see their legs. I like looking at
them when I play. The sight of their knees moving and their feet
tapping in time to the music.'

'Why did she give you the letter? It has stamps on it.'

'She wasn't wearing heels. She wore flat boots, and they were covered in mud. Poor people's boots. She looked better than when you introduced her to me here.'

'Why did she want you to give me the letter?'

'I suppose I lied to her. She wanted you to get it as soon as possible. She opened her bag and took out cigarettes, lipstick, a handkerchief, all those absurd things women carry around. She laid it all out on the dressing table and searched for the letter. She even had a gun. She didn't take it out of the bag, but I saw it.'

'A gun?'

'A shiny thirty-eight. There's nothing a woman won't carry around in her bag. At last she found the letter. And I lied to her. She wanted me to. I told her I'd be seeing you in a couple of weeks. But then I left the club and there was all that business in New York . . . Maybe I wasn't lying at the time. I was thinking of coming to see you and I just got on the wrong plane. But I didn't lose your letter. I kept it in the false bottom, like in the old days . . .'

The following day Biralbo went to see Billy Swann off at the station feeling slightly bereft but also relieved. In the station hall, in the cafeteria, on the platform, they exchanged false promises: Billy Swann would give up alcohol for a while, Biralbo would send a blasphemous letter of resignation to the nuns, they'd meet in Stockholm in two or three weeks' time, and Biralbo wouldn't send any more letters to Berlin, because there was no better way to get over a woman than to forget her. But after the train left, Biralbo sat in the cafeteria and re-read Lucrecia's letter for the sixth or seventh time, trying unsuccessfully not to feel saddened by its cold, hurried tone. It contained ten or twelve lines written on the back of a map of Lisbon. She said she'd be back soon and apologized for not having found anything else to write on. The map was a blurred photocopy with a point marked in red towards the left and a word written in a hand that wasn't Lucrecia's: *Burma*.

To understand why Floro Bloom kept the Lady Bird open you had to take into account his laziness and propensity for the more pointless forms of loyalty. His real name, apparently, was Floreal, and he came from a family of Republicans. Around 1970 he was living happily somewhere in Canada, having escaped political persecution which he never talked about. As for the nickname Bloom, I have reason to believe it was given to him by Santiago Biralbo, because Floro was slow and ponderous and had round, pink cheeks, like an apple. He was fat and blond, and looked more like a Canadian or a Swede than a Spaniard. His memories, like his external life, were comfortingly simple. After a couple of drinks he'd start reminiscing about a restaurant in Quebec where he worked for a few months, a sort of outdoor snack bar in the middle of a forest, where squirrels came and licked the plates and were quite tame. They twitched their little damp noses, their tiny claws and tails, and then bounded away over the grass. They knew exactly when to return in the evening to catch the leftovers, and sometimes one of them even came and sat on the table while you were eating. Standing behind the bar of the Lady Bird with tears in his eyes, Floro Bloom could picture them as clearly as if they were in front of him now. They weren't frightened at all, he'd say, as if it were an amazing thing. They licked his hand, like kittens; they were happy squirrels. But then Floro Bloom would become as solemn as the allegory of the Republic hanging in the back room of the Lady Bird and make pronouncements: 'Imagine what would happen here if a squirrel came and sat on a table in a restaurant. They'd cut its head off, for sure, or stab it with a fork.'

That summer, thanks to all the tourists, the Lady Bird enjoyed a fragile golden age. Floro Bloom found it all a little trying; weary and anxious, he had to serve at tables as well as the bar, which left him almost no time to chat to his regulars, meaning those of us who only paid from time to time. He stood behind the bar and looked round in astonishment, watching his home being overrun by strangers, but he overcame his personal distaste to play the records requested and listened with placid indifference to the confessions of drunkards who spoke only English. Perhaps, when he looked most lost, he was thinking of the tame little squirrels in Quebec.

He hired a waiter and sat at the till practising a look of deep concentration, which allowed him to avoid dealing with anyone he didn't care for. For a couple of months, until the beginning of September, Santiago Biralbo went back to playing the piano at the Lady Bird, enjoying unlimited credit in bottles of bourbon. Out of shyness or a foreboding of failure, I've never been able to

drink in empty bars, and that summer I returned to the Lady Bird.
I chose a secluded corner, drank alone, and maybe discussed the
Republic's Law on Religious Worship with Floro Bloom. When
Biralbo finished his set we would have a last drink together, and at
dawn walk back into town following the curve of lights around the
bay. One evening, as I sat in my usual place with a drink in front of
me, Floro Bloom came over and wiped down the bar staring at
something behind me.

'Turn round and have a look at the blonde,' he said. 'You won't
forget her.'

But she wasn't alone. Her long, straight hair fell about her shoulders, shining like pale gold. The skin at her temples was
translucent, showing the veins beneath. Her eyes were blue and
expressionless; looking at her was like surrendering willingly to the
chill of disgrace. She rested her hands on her long thighs and
moved in time to the tune Biralbo was playing, but didn't otherwise
seem interested in the music, or in Floro Bloom's gaze, or mine, or
the existence of anybody else. She watched Biralbo as indifferently as a statue staring out to sea, occasionally sipping her drink,
or giving replies as trivial as comments on an etching to the man
sitting next to her.

'They've been here for the past two or three nights,' Floro Bloom
informed me. 'They sit, order drinks and stare at Biralbo. But he
hasn't noticed. He's got only one thing on his mind – he's planning
on going to Stockholm with Billy Swann, and all he thinks about is
music.'

'And Lucrecia,' I said with the flawless perception one has in
judging other people's lives.

'Who can tell?' said Floro Bloom. 'Look at that blonde, though.
And what about the guy who's with her.'

He was so tall and vulgar that it took a moment to notice that he was also black. He smiled constantly, at nothing in particular. They would drink a great deal and leave when the music was over, always tipping generously. One evening he stood next to me at the bar, ordering drinks. He had a cigar between his teeth and exhaled vigorously through his nose, for a moment enveloping me in smoke. At a table at the back, the blonde sat waiting for him, leaning against the wall, looking bored and alone. He stood staring at me, a drink in each hand, and said he knew me. A mutual friend had mentioned me. 'Malcolm,' he said, chewing on his cigar and putting the drinks down as if to give me time to remember. 'Bruce Malcolm,' he repeated in the strangest accent I'd ever heard. He waved the smoke away from his face. 'But I think he was known as the American here.'

He spoke with what sounded like a parody of a French accent. He sounded exactly like a film-Negro, saying 'de American' and 'I tink', and he smiled at Floro Bloom and me as if we were his life-long friends. He asked who the piano player was and repeated admiringly: 'Bigalbo.' He was wearing a leather jacket. The skin of his hands was pale and smooth like well-worn leather and his hair was greying. There seemed to be constant approval in his large, placid eyes. Nodding a lot, he asked us to excuse him and picked up his drinks. With obvious pride, and humility, he said his secretary was waiting for him. By some miracle he managed to deposit his card on the bar without relinquishing the drinks or removing the cigar from his mouth. Floro Bloom and I peered at it. It read: *Toussaints Morton, Paintings and Antiquarian Books, Berlin.*

'So you met them all,' Biralbo said in Madrid. 'Malcolm, Lucrecia. Even Toussaints Morton.'

'It wasn't too hard,' I said. I didn't mind Biralbo making fun of me, smiling as though he knew everything. 'We lived in the same town, went to the same bars.'

'And knew the same women. Do you remember his secretary?'

'Floro Bloom was right. Once you'd seen her you never forgot her. But she was like an ice carving. Her veins showed blue under her skin.'

'She was a bitch,' Biralbo said suddenly. He didn't usually use that kind of language. 'Do you remember the way she looked at me at the Lady Bird? Well, that's exactly how she looked when Malcolm and her boss were about to kill me, in Lisbon, less than a year ago.'

Instantly he seemed to regret saying this. It was often his tactic, or habit, to say something and then look away and smile, as if giving you the choice not to believe him. After that his face would look as it did when he was playing at the Metropolitano, drowsy, or maybe cold – calm, contemptuous witness to his own music and words, which were as fleeting and unquestionable as a melody. He didn't mention Toussaints Morton or his blonde secretary again until the last time we saw each other, in his hotel room. He was holding a revolver and looking out through the curtains. He didn't seem scared. He just waited, motionless, watching the street, the people gathering on the corner by the Telefónica building, as vigilant as when counting the days since Lucrecia's last letter.

He hadn't known it then, but Billy Swann's arrival was a portent of Lucrecia's return. A few weeks after Billy left, Toussaints Morton appeared; he too came from Berlin, that unimaginable place where Lucrecia still existed as a real being.

In my memory, that summer is distilled in a few afternoons of indolence, purple and pink skies in the distance above the sea, and long evenings where the drinks were as tepid as the gentle

dawn rain. As evening fell, slim, foreign blondes came to the Lady
Bird, still with their beach bags and sandals, skin slightly pink from
the sun and a light crust of salt on their thighs. At the bar, Floro
Bloom considered them with silent tenderness, like fawns, as he
served them drinks. He made imaginary selections, pointing out to
me this one's profile or that one's eyes – encouraging signs perhaps.
I can remember them all, including the ones who stayed on a
couple of evenings with Floro Bloom and me after he closed the
Lady Bird, rough drafts of the model that possessed all the perfect
features scattered among those women – Toussaints Morton's tall,
ice-cold secretary.

Biralbo didn't notice her at first. He didn't think about women
much then, and when Floro Bloom or I told him to look at one that
particularly attracted us, he took pleasure in pointing out her minor
defects: stubby hands, for instance, or ankles that were too thick.
The third or fourth evening, she arrived with Toussaints Morton at
their usual time and sat at the same table, near the stage. Glancing
round at the regulars, Biralbo was surprised to find something in
her face that reminded him of Lucrecia. It made him look at her
several times, searching for the same expression again, but it never
reappeared and may never have been there, the vestige of a time
when he sought an echo of Lucrecia's features, her expression, her
walk, in all women.

That summer, he told me two years later, he began to realize
that music had to be a cold, absolute passion. He was playing reg-
ularly again, mostly at the Lady Bird and nearly always solo, and he
felt the music flowing through his fingers like a river as endless and
serene as time. He gave himself up to it as if surrendering to the
speed of a car, moving ever faster, dedicated to darkness and distance, governed only by his instinct to get away, to escape, seeing

no further than the stretch of road lit by the headlights, like driving alone at midnight along an unfamiliar road. Until then his music had been a confession, always addressed to somebody – to Lucrecia, to himself. Now, he sensed that music was becoming a way of predicting the future. He'd almost lost the habit of wondering, as he played, what Lucrecia would think if she could hear him. Slowly his ghosts abandoned him to his solitude. Sometimes, soon after waking in the morning, he realized to his surprise that there had been a few minutes when he hadn't thought of her. Even in dreams he didn't see her: she always had her back to him, or she was against the light so her face was always denied him, or turned out to be somebody else's. In his dreams he often wandered at night through a fantastical Berlin full of illuminated skyscrapers, and red and blue lights above streets burnished by frost, but it was an empty city and Lucrecia wasn't there.

At the beginning of June he wrote her a final letter. A month later, when he opened his letterbox, he found what he hadn't seen for a long time, what he now only expected out of a habit more deep-rooted than will: a long, slim envelope with striped edges. He tore it open and only then realized that it was the letter he had sent to Lucrecia a few weeks earlier. There was a red scrawl – a signature perhaps – and a sentence in German on the back. Somebody at the Lady Bird translated it for him: 'Not known at this address.'

He re-read the letter that had travelled so far only to return to him. He thought without bitterness that he'd spent almost three years writing to himself, and it was time to live a different life. For the first time since meeting Lucrecia he dared to imagine what the world would be like if she didn't exist, or if he'd never met her. But only when he went on stage at the Lady Bird, with a whisky or two inside him, did he truly sink into oblivion, into empty elation.

And then one evening in July he saw a face that acted on his
memory like a hand touching a scar, bringing back the raw pain of
the wound.

Toussaints Morton's secretary stared at him as if he were a wall
or a motionless landscape. He saw her again a few hours later,
waiting for the Mole. The platform was dirty and dimly lit, with
the feeling of desolation stations always have just before dawn. But
the blonde sat there, a leather handbag and a folder in her lap,
remote and serene, as if in an elegant salon. Beside her, Toussaints
Morton chewed on a cigar and smiled at the filthy walls and
Biralbo, who didn't recognize him. Distrusting the friendliness of
strangers, Biralbo chose to ignore the smile and the possibility
that it was a greeting. He bought a ticket and stood waiting for the
train. He could hear the man and woman talking quietly behind
him, in a seamless mixture of French and English he found incomprehensible. From time to time the man's laughter interrupted their
whispering and echoed loudly around the deserted station. With a
stab of anxiety Biralbo thought the man might be laughing at him,
but couldn't bring himself to look round. In the silence that followed he was sure they were staring at him. The train arrived but
they didn't move. Once inside, Biralbo looked at them openly
through the window and was met with Toussaints Morton's
obscene smile and nod of farewell. He saw them stand as the Mole
slowly left the station and assumed they got on the train two or
three carriages back, because he didn't see them again that evening.
Perhaps they were heading for the frontier at Irún; by the time he
opened his front door he'd forgotten all about them.

Some men are immune to ridicule, entirely unaware they appear
intent on turning themselves into a parody. At the time I considered Toussaints Morton one of them. He was very tall and

high-heeled boots made him seem taller still. He wore leather
jackets and pink shirts with pointed collars so long they almost
reached his shoulders. Rings set with highly dubious stones
adorned his fingers, and gold chains shone against his dark, hairy
chest. He grinned broadly, chewing on a foul-smelling cigar, and
cleaned his nails with the long, gold toothpick he always kept in
his breast pocket, afterwards sniffing them discreetly, as if taking
snuff. An indefinable smell preceded and followed him, a combi-
nation of cigar smoke and the perfume that enveloped his
secretary, seeming to emanate from her straight hair, her stillness,
her translucent skin.

Now, years later, I remember that smell, which always conjured
up the past and a certain fear. Santiago Biralbo noticed it for the
first time one summer afternoon, in San Sebastian, in the hall of his
block of flats. He'd risen very late and eaten in a bar near by; the
Lady Bird was closed on Wednesdays so he wasn't going into town
that evening. He was heading towards the lift holding the key to
his letterbox, which he still checked several times a day, in case the
postman was late, when a strange feeling of remote familiarity
made him stiffen and look round: before he could identify the perfume he saw Toussaints Morton and his secretary sitting cheerfully
on the sofa in the hall. On the secretary's bare knees lay the same
handbag and folder that he'd seen a few days earlier at the station.
Toussaints Morton cradled a large paper bag from which protruded
the neck of a whisky bottle. He smiled almost fiercely, a cigar
clamped firmly to one side of his mouth. Standing, he removed the
cigar and held out a large hand to Biralbo. It felt like wood worn
smooth with use. The secretary – called Daphne, Biralbo later discovered – made an almost human gesture as she stood up: shaking
her hair off her face, she smiled at Biralbo, but only with her lips.

Toussaints Morton spoke Spanish like someone driving at full speed, entirely ignoring the highway code and thumbing his nose at the police. Neither grammatical rules nor embarrassment ever dimmed his enthusiasm. When he couldn't think of a word he bit his lips, said 'shit' and switched to another language like a smuggler slipping across the border. He apologized to Biralbo for 'bodering' him and declared himself a great fan of jazz, of Art Tatum, of Billy Swann, of relaxing evenings at the Lady Bird. He said he preferred the intimacy of small clubs to the obvious foolishness of mass entertainment — jazz, like flamenco, was a minority interest. He introduced himself and his secretary, saying he ran a flourishing antiques business in Berlin, discreet and — he hinted — clandestine: the taxes were crippling if you opened a shop with a big sign out- side. He gestured vaguely at his secretary's folder, and the paper bag he himself was holding. In Berlin, London, New York — Biralbo had no doubt heard of the Nathan Levy Gallery — Toussaints Morton was well known in the engravings and antiquarian books business.

Daphne sat there placidly, as if listening to falling rain. Biralbo opened the lift door and was about to go up to his flat on the eighth floor in a slight daze, as usual after spending many hours alone, when Toussaints Morton stopped the door with his knee and said, with a big smile, cigar in his mouth: 'Lucrecia talked about you a great deal in Berlin. We were great friends. She always said: "When I have no one left, I'll still have Santiago Biralbo."'

Biralbo said nothing. They followed him into the lift and stood in an awkward silence mitigated only by Toussaints Morton's immutable smile and the blue gaze of his secretary, which she fixed on the floor numbers lighting up in quick succession as if looking at a view of the city, serene in the distance. Biralbo didn't ask them in but they came anyway. Smiling, curious, they walked down the hall of his flat as though visiting a small provincial museum, examining everything approvingly – the pictures, the lamps and the sofa, where they immediately sat down. Biralbo found himself standing in front of them, not knowing what to say, as though he'd come home to find them chatting on the sofa in the dining room and couldn't think how to get rid of them, or ask them why they were there. After many hours alone his sense of reality became especially fragile. For a moment he felt lost, as in a dream, picturing himself in front of two strangers who occupied his sofa, intrigued not by the reason for their presence but by the inscription on Toussaints Morton's gold medallion. He asked them if they wanted a drink and then remembered he didn't have anything to offer them. Smiling happily, Toussaints Morton half uncovered his bottle and pointed at the label with his thick index finger – he had the hands of a double-bass player.

'Lucrecia always said, "My friend Biralbo drinks only the best bourbon." I wonder if this is good enough for you. Daphne found it and told me, "Toussaints, it's expensive, but you won't find a better one even in Tennessee." But the fact is, Daphne doesn't drink. She doesn't smoke either, and she only eats vegetables and boiled fish. You tell him, Daphne, the gentleman speaks English. She's very shy. She says to me, "Toussaints, how can you talk so much and in so many languages?" And I tell her, "Because I have to say everything that you don't!"'

Toussaints Morton leaned backwards as if propelled by laughter, and placed a large, dark hand on Daphne's white knees. Upright, serene, she smiled slightly.

'I like this place.' Toussaints Morton glanced eagerly, happily round the near-empty dining room, as if gratefully receiving hospitality he'd long wished for. The records, furniture, that piano. When I was a child my mother wanted me to learn to play. "Toussaints," she said, "some day you'll thank me for it." But I never learned. Lucrecia always talked about this place. Good taste, simplicity. The moment I saw you the other night, I said to Daphne, "He and Lucrecia are soulmates." I know a man by looking into his eyes just once. But with women it's different. Daphne's been my secretary for four years, and do you think I know her? No more than I know the President of the United States . . .'

'But Lucrecia's never been here,' thought Biralbo distantly. Toussaints Morton's laughter and ceaseless chatter had a soporific effect on him. He was still standing. He said he was going to fetch glasses and some ice. When he asked if they wanted water, Toussaints Morton put his hand over his mouth as if he couldn't restrain his laughter.

'Of course we want water. Daphne and I always order whisky and water in bars. Water for her, and whisky for me.'

When Biralbo returned from the kitchen Toussaints Morton was standing by the piano, leafing through a book. He snapped it shut, smiling, pretending to look apologetic. For an instant Biralbo glimpsed a cold, searching look in Toussaints Morton's eyes – large, dead eyes, rimmed with red – that didn't fit the rest of his performance. Daphne stared at her nails, her hands palms down in her lap. They were long and pink, unvarnished, slightly paler than her skin.

'Allow me,' said Toussaints Morton. He took the tray from Biralbo and filled two glasses with bourbon, making as if to pour one for Daphne before suddenly remembering she didn't drink. Noisily savouring his first gulp, he put the glass on the table beside the telephone. He sat back in the sofa comfortably, almost as though he was the host, and re-lit his cigar contentedly.

'I knew it,' he said. 'I knew exactly what you were like even before I saw you. Ask Daphne. I always said to her, "Daphne, Malcolm isn't right for Lucrecia. Not while that piano player back in Spain is alive." Lucrecia talked so much about you, out in Berlin . . . When Malcolm wasn't around, of course. Daphne and I were like a family to her when they separated. Daphne'll tell you: Lucrecia was always welcome to a meal and a bed at my place. It wasn't a good time for her.'

'When did she split up with Malcolm?' asked Biralbo. Toussaints Morton looked at him with the same expression that had so chilled Biralbo when he returned from the kitchen, but immediately burst out laughing.

'Do you hear that, Daphne? The gentleman acts surprised. That's not necessary, my friend, you two no longer have to keep it a secret, not in front of me. Do you know that it was I who sometimes posted Lucrecia's letters to you? I, Toussaints Morton. Malcolm loved her, he was my friend, but I could see that she was crazy about you. Daphne and I often talked about it. I'd say to her, "Daphne, Malcolm is my friend and partner but that girl has a right to fall in love with whoever she wants." That was my opinion. You can ask Daphne, there are no secrets between us.'

Toussaints Morton's words were beginning to have the same effect on Biralbo as bourbon, making everything seem unreal. Without him noticing, they had already drunk more than half the bottle, with Toussaints Morton sloshing bourbon into the glasses, and over the tray and the table, wiping up large spills immediately with a handkerchief as long and brightly coloured as a magician's. Biralbo had suspected from the start that he was lying and now he began to listen with the attention of a slightly unscrupulous jeweller buying stolen goods for the first time.

'I don't know anything about Lucrecia,' he said. 'I haven't seen her for three years.'

'He doesn't trust us.' Toussaints Morton shook his head sadly and looked at his secretary as if seeking solace from Biralbo's ingratitude. 'Do you see, Daphne? Just like Lucrecia. I'm not surprised, sir.' He turned back to Biralbo, dignified and serious, but he had that same look in his eyes, indifferent to games and fakery. 'She didn't trust us either. You tell him, Daphne. Tell him how she left Berlin without a word to us.'

'She's not living in Berlin?'

But Toussaints Morton didn't answer. He got to his feet with visible difficulty, and leant on the back of the sofa panting, his cigar hanging from the corner of his mouth. His secretary automatically stood up too, cradling the folder in her arms and her handbag on her shoulder. As she moved her perfume – with hints of smoke and ash – spread through the air.

'Very well, sir,' said Toussaints Morton, looking hurt and disappointed. Biralbo was again struck by how tall he was. 'I understand. I understand if Lucrecia doesn't want to have anything to do with us. Old friends mean nothing nowadays. But please tell her that Toussaints Morton was here and would like to see her. Tell her that.'

Biralbo felt a ridiculous urge to apologize. He said again that he hadn't heard from Lucrecia, she wasn't in San Sebastian, maybe she hadn't come back to Spain. Toussaints Morton's calm and inebriated eyes were fixed on him like on the proof of a lie, an unnecessary betrayal. Before getting in the lift he handed Biralbo a card: they weren't returning to Berlin just yet, he said, they'd be spending a few weeks in Spain, so if Lucrecia changed her mind and wanted to see them, here was their telephone number in

Madrid. Biralbo remained alone on the landing, and when he went back inside locked the door behind him. He couldn't hear the rumble of the lift, but Toussaints Morton's cigar smoke and his secretary's perfume remained thick in the air.

'Look,' said Biralbo. 'Look at the way he's smiling.'

I went over to the window, parted the curtains slightly and looked out. Across the street, motionless and taller than the passers-by, Toussaints Morton watched and smiled as if he approved of everything: the Madrid night, the cold, the women standing on the pavement near him, smoking and leaning against street signs or the wall of the Telefónica building.

'Does he know we're here?' I moved away from the window – I had the feeling I'd been seen.

'Yes,' said Biralbo. 'He wants me to see him. He wants me to know he's found me.'

'Why doesn't he come up?'

'Pride. To scare me. He's been there for two days.'

'I can't see his secretary.'

'Maybe he sent her to the Metropolitano. In case I leave by the back door. I know him. He doesn't want to catch me yet. For now, he just wants me to know I can't escape.'

'I'll turn the light off.'

'It makes no difference. He'll know we're still here.'

Biralbo closed the curtains and sat down on the bed, holding the revolver. The room seemed smaller and darker in the dingy light of the bedside lamps. The telephone rang. An old-fashioned model, black, sharp-cornered, funereal, it looked as if it had been designed solely for relaying bad news. Biralbo kept it close: he stared at it and then looked at me as it rang, but didn't answer. I wished for each ring to be the last, but after a second's silence it would sound again, even more piercing and persistent, as though we'd been listening to it for hours. Finally I picked up the receiver and asked who was calling. There was no answer, only an intermittent, high-pitched whistle. Biralbo didn't move from the bed. He was smoking, not even looking in my direction, and he started whistling a slow tune, exhaling smoke. I looked out of the window. Toussaints Morton was no longer there.

'He'll be back,' said Biralbo. 'He always is.'

'What does he want from you?'

'Something I don't have.'

'Are you going to the Metropolitano?'

'I don't feel like playing tonight. Call and ask for Monica. Tell her I'm ill.'

It was insanely hot in the room and hot air hummed in the air conditioning, but Biralbo kept his coat on, as if he really was ill. When I think of him during those final days I always picture him in that coat, stretched out on the bed, or smoking at the window,

his right hand in the pocket of his overcoat, searching for cigarettes or maybe the butt of his revolver. He kept a couple of
bottles of whisky in the wardrobe. We drank methodically, without attention or pleasure, from opaque bathroom glasses. The
neat whisky burnt my lips, but I went on drinking and said
almost nothing, listening to Biralbo and looking out occasionally
across the Gran Vía, searching for the tall figure of Toussaints
Morton; as night fell, I shivered whenever it seemed that one of
the dark-skinned men pausing at street corners might be him.
Fear rose up towards me from the street like the sound of distant
sirens. I felt exposed to the elements, alone in a cold winter
wind, as if the walls and closed doors of the hotel could no
longer protect me.

But Biralbo wasn't afraid. He didn't care what was happening,
across the street, or maybe much closer, just outside his door, in the
hotel corridors – muffled footsteps and a key turning in a lock, an
anonymous, invisible hotel guest who could later be heard coughing in the room next door. Biralbo cleaned his revolver repeatedly,
casually, the way one might shine a pair of shoes. I remember the
brand inscribed on the barrel: Colt Trooper .38. It had a strange
beauty, like a newly sharpened knife, and its gleaming form seemed
unreal, as if it wasn't a weapon that could suddenly go off and kill
someone but a symbol, lethal and still, like a bottle of poison kept
in a cupboard.

It had belonged to Lucrecia. She brought it back from Berlin,
part of her new identity, like her very long hair and dark glasses
and unspoken desire for stealth and constant escape. By the
time she returned Biralbo had given up waiting for her: she
emerged, not out of the past or from the imaginary Berlin of her
letters and postcards, but from pure absence, from the void,

with a new identity barely perceptible in her old face, like the foreign intonation she now gave certain words. She returned one November morning – Biralbo was woken by the telephone and at first didn't recognize Lucrecia's voice. He'd forgotten what she sounded like, just as he'd forgotten the exact colour of her eyes.

'One-thirty,' she said. 'At that bar on the Paseo Maritimo. La Gaviota. Do you remember?'

Biralbo didn't remember. He hung up and looked at the alarm clock as if still in a dream – it was half past twelve, a grey day made doubly strange by not going to work and by hearing Lucrecia's voice, still fresh, returned, almost unrecognizable but after all their years of distance no longer unattainable. Now she occupied a precise point in reality, at a time in the near future – one-thirty, she said, and then the name of a bar and a conventional farewell confirming that she now belonged to the realm of possible meetings, and of faces one no longer needed to imagine because a simple telephone call would summon them. Time began to pass for Biralbo at a speed he'd never known before and it made him clumsy, as though he was trying to keep up with musicians playing too quickly. His own slowness affected everything around him – he thought the water heater in the shower would never come to life, and clean clothes seemed to have vanished from the wardrobe; the lift was in use and took an eternity to reach his floor, there were no taxis to be found, and the railway station was deserted.

He noticed that all these minor setbacks distracted him from Lucrecia. Fifteen minutes before her three-year absence was to end, as Biralbo searched for a taxi, she was further than ever from his thoughts. Only when he told the driver where he was going did he remember with a shiver that he would soon be seeing her as clearly as he could see his own frightened eyes in the rear-view mirror. But the face in the mirror wasn't his. The features seemed unfamiliar – it was the face that Lucrecia would see and search for signs of time's passing, which Biralbo himself noticed only now, looking at himself through her eyes.

Even before meeting her, he felt drawn by her invisible presence, because haste and fear were also part of Lucrecia for him, along with the feeling of abandoning himself to the taxi's speed as he used to when risking a secret, half-hour meeting with her. It struck him that in the last three years time had stood still, as with space when travelling across a vast plain at night. Time had been measured by the intervals between Lucrecia's letters, and all the other events in his life seemed in his careless memory merely figures on a bas-relief, or the dents and marks on the wall he stared at when he couldn't sleep at night. Now, in the taxi, every detail was unique, swept away by time, dissolved in it; imperious time that once more demanded to be measured in minutes, or even split seconds, by the clock on the dashboard in front of him, or the church clock he passed at twenty-past one, or the watch he pictured on Lucrecia's wrist, as secret and regular as the beating of her heart. He had regained the astonishing certainty that Lucrecia existed, but with it the fear of being late, and of having put on weight and appearing debased, of being unworthy of his memory of her or unfaithful to the predictions of his imagination.

The taxi entered the city, driving down the tree-lined avenues beside the river, across the Avenida de los Tamarindos and through the damp, narrow streets of the Parte Vieja, emerging suddenly on to the Paseo Maritimo, under a huge expanse of grey sky where suicidal gulls wheeled in the drizzle. A man, alone, in a dark coat and a hat pulled down over his face, stood by the handrail, staring dully out to sea as if watching the end of the world. In front of him, waves broke against the rocks sending spray high into the air. Biralbo thought he saw the man shielding a cigarette from the wind in the hollow of his hand. He thought: 'I am that man.' The bar where Lucrecia had arranged to meet him was on a promontory. He caught sight of its gleaming windows as the taxi rounded a bend. Suddenly Biralbo's whole life was compressed into the two minutes that remained before the taxi stopped. Seagulls bobbed on the grey crests of the waves reminding Biralbo of the man in the dark coat – he and the gulls seemed indifferent in the face of disaster. But it was just another way of avoiding the terrifying thought that in only a few seconds' time he would be seeing Lucrecia. The taxi driver drew up by the side of the road and stared at Biralbo in the rear-view mirror. 'La Gaviota,' he said solemnly. 'We're here.'

Despite the large windows at the back, La Gaviota had an opacity suggesting secret rendezvous, whisky after hours and restrained alcoholism. The automatic doors opened silently before Biralbo. He saw clean, empty tables with checked tablecloths, and a very long, deserted bar. On the other side of the windows was the island crowned by the lighthouse, beyond that the cliffs and the sea stretching grey into the distance, and the dark green hills draped with mist. Calmly, as if he were someone else, he remembered the title of a song: 'Stormy Weather'. It reminded him of Lucrecia.

He thought he must be late, that he had mistaken the time or the place. Sitting side-on to the view that was occasionally obscured by spray, a woman sat smoking, a large, clear glass untouched before her. Her face was hidden by very long hair and dark glasses. She stood, removing her glasses. 'Lucrecia,' said Biralbo, still not moving. He wasn't calling to her, he simply named her in disbelief.

I don't picture these scenes clearly, or search for the details behind Biralbo's words. I see them as if from a great distance, with a precision that owes nothing to any effort of will or memory. I see their slow embrace in the pale light of a San Sebastian day, as if just then I was walking along the Paseo Maritimo and caught a glimpse, through the windows, of a man and a woman together in a deserted bar. I see it all from the future, from those evenings spent drinking warily in Biralbo's hotel room, when he told me about Lucrecia's return, trying to temper his account with an irony that was betrayed by the expression in his eyes, by the revolver on the bedside table.

As Biralbo kissed Lucrecia he noticed an unfamiliar smell in her hair. He stood back to look at her, and what he saw was not the face that his memory had blurred for three years, or the eyes whose colour he could never recall, but a confirmation that time had passed. She was much thinner, and her long, dark hair and fatigue sharpened her features. A face is a prediction that always comes true. Hers seemed more foreign and beautiful than ever because it had fulfilled Biralbo's old expectations, and made his love spread over her. In the past Lucrecia had dressed in bright colours and worn her hair shoulder length. Now she wore very tight black trousers, accentuating her thinness, and a short grey coat. She smoked American cigarettes and drank faster than Biralbo, emptying her glass with masculine determination. She kept her dark glasses on. When Biralbo asked her what 'Burma' meant she burst out laughing. 'Nothing,' she said. 'A place in Lisbon.' She'd used the back of a photocopied map because she felt like writing to him and couldn't find any paper.

'You never felt like writing again,' said Biralbo, smiling to soften the useless reproach in his voice.

'I did, every day.' Lucrecia pushed her hair off her face and held it back with her hands pressed to her temples. 'Every day and every minute, all I could think of was writing to you. I was talking to you even though I didn't write, telling you everything that was happening to me as it happened. All of it, even the worst things. Even the ones I didn't want to know myself. You stopped writing to me too.'

'Only when one of my letters was returned.'

'I left Berlin.'

'In January?'

'How did you know?' Lucrecia smiled. She toyed with an unlit cigarette and her sunglasses. In her eyes there was a distance more grey and final than that of the town laid out around the bay, stretching beyond the hills into the mist.

'That's when Billy Swann saw you.'

'You remember everything. I was always frightened by how good your memory was.'

'You didn't say you were thinking of leaving Malcolm.'

'I wasn't: one morning I simply woke up and left. He still can't believe it.'

'Is he still in Berlin?'

'I suppose so.' In Lucrecia's eyes there was a resolve that left no room for doubt or fear; or mercy, thought Biralbo. 'I haven't heard from him since I left.'

'Where did you go?' Biralbo was afraid to ask. He knew he was approaching the line he didn't dare go beyond. Holding his gaze, Lucrecia remained silent. She didn't need to say anything or even shake her head, she could deny something just by looking into his eyes.

'I wanted to go any place where he wasn't. Him or his friends.'

'One of them was here,' said Biralbo slowly. 'Toussaints Morton.'

Alarm flashed across Lucrecia's face but her gaze remained steady. For an instant she looked around as though frightened she might see Toussaints Morton sitting at a nearby table, or leaning his elbows on the bar, smiling through the smoke of one of his stubby cigars.

'This summer, in July,' Biralbo went on. 'He thought you were here in San Sebastian. He said you and he were great friends.'

'He's nobody's friend, not even Malcolm's.'

'He was sure you were with me,' said Biralbo sadly, shyly, but then changed his tone immediately. 'Does he have business with Malcolm?'

'He works alone, with his secretary, Daphne. He sometimes employs Malcolm. Malcolm's never been half as important as he makes out.'

'Did he threaten you?'

'Malcolm?'

'When you told him you were leaving.'

'He didn't say a word. He didn't believe it. He couldn't believe that a woman would leave him. He's probably still waiting for me.'

'Billy Swann thought you were scared of something.'

'Billy Swann drinks too much.' Lucrecia smiled in a way that Biralbo had never seen before, like the way she emptied her glass and held her cigarette – signs that time had passed, that they were now almost strangers, and that their loyalty towards each other had burnt itself out. 'You can't imagine how happy I was when I heard he was in Berlin. I didn't want to hear him play, I just wanted him to tell me about you.'

'He's in Copenhagen now. He called me the other day. He hasn't had a drink in six months.'

'Why aren't you there with him?'

'I had to wait for you.'

'I'm not staying in San Sebastian.'

'Nor am I. I can leave now.'

'You didn't even know if I'd be back.'

'Maybe you're not back.'

'Yes, I am. I'm here. I'm Lucrecia. You're Santiago Biralbo.'

Lucrecia reached across the table and took hold of Biralbo's hands. He didn't grip back. She touched his face and hair, as if seeking stronger confirmation than her eyes alone could provide that it was him. She felt, perhaps not tenderness, but a sense that they were both orphaned. Two years later, in Lisbon, through a winter's night and on until dawn, Biralbo was to learn that this one thing would link them for ever – not desire or memory, but abandonment, the certainty that they were alone, without even the excuse of a love gone awry.

Lucrecia glanced at her watch, without saying that she had to go. It was almost the only gesture that he recognized, the only anxiety that came back to him intact. But now there was no Malcolm, no need for haste or secrecy. Lucrecia gathered her cigarettes and lighter and put on her sunglasses.

'Do you still play at the Lady Bird?'

'Very rarely. But I can play there tonight if you like. Floro Bloom would be pleased to see you. He always asked me about you.'

'I don't want to go to the Lady Bird,' said Lucrecia, already standing and zipping up her coat. 'I don't want to go anywhere that'll remind me of those times.'

They didn't kiss as they parted. Just as he had three years before, Biralbo watched her taxi drive away, but this time Lucrecia didn't turn to look back.

He walked slowly back into town along the Paseo Maritimo, splashed from time to time by the cold spray from waves breaking against the rocks. The man in the dark coat and hat was still there, staring at the seagulls. Biralbo descended the Aquarium stairs to the port, hungry, dazed, slightly drunk, propelled by an agitation that resembled neither joy nor unhappiness, but which preceded or was indifferent to such emotions, like the desire to eat or smoke a cigarette. As he walked he whispered the words to a song that Lucrecia had always liked, which had been like a password for them, and a shameless declaration of love. When she and Malcolm arrived at the Lady Bird, Biralbo would start to play it — not the whole thing, just hints, sprinkling a few unmistakable notes through another melody. He realized now that the song no longer moved him. It had lost its link to Lucrecia, to the past, even to him.

He remembered something Billy Swann had said: 'Music doesn't
care about us. It doesn't care how much pain or passion we put into
it when we play or listen. It uses us, like a woman with a lover she's
indifferent to.'

He was meeting Lucrecia for dinner that evening. 'Take me
somewhere new,' she'd said, 'somewhere I've never been.' She
sounded like she meant a foreign country rather than a restaurant,
but she'd always talked like that, applying a kind of heroic craving
and impossible desire to the most banal episodes in her life. He
would be seeing her again at nine o'clock. The bells near Santa
María del Mar had just struck three. Time was as stifling as the
hotel rooms where, three years before, he used to meet Lucrecia.
She would leave him facing the unmade bed and the view of the
motionless sea from the window. On winter afternoons in San
Sebastian the sea in the distance is like a horizontal expanse of
slate. He wandered through the arcades, between piles of nets and
empty fish crates. He felt vaguely comforted by the colours of the
houses, muted in the grey afternoon, with their blue façades and
green or red shutters, and by the line of roofs stretching up into the
hills in the distance. While Lucrecia was away the city had not
existed for him; but now, with her return, he could see it once
more. Even the silence emphasizing the sound of his footsteps and
the smells of the port confirmed that Lucrecia was near.

Biralbo didn't remember that we had eaten together that day. I
was having lunch with Floro Bloom in a tavern in the Parte Vieja
when I saw him come in slowly, absorbed in his own thoughts, his
hair wet, and sit at a table at the back. 'The Vatican's lackey no
longer wishes to mix with the world's pariahs,' Floro Bloom said
loudly, turning towards him. Biralbo brought his beer over to our
table, but hardly said a word throughout the meal. I know it was

the day he saw Lucrecia because he blushed slightly when Floro asked him if he really was ill: that morning Floro had rung the school to talk to Biralbo, and somebody said — in a clerical-sounding voice — that Mr Santiago Biralbo was not in class because he was indisposed. 'Indisposed,' stressed Floro Bloom. 'Only a nun would talk like that nowadays.' Biralbo ate quickly and apologized for not staying to have coffee with us — his train was leaving at four. When he'd left, Floro Bloom shook his heavy, bear-like head. 'He denies it,' he said, 'but I'm sure those nuns make him recite the rosary.'

Biralbo didn't go to work that afternoon either. When he gave up believing he had a future as a musician and grew used to the indignity of teaching music theory, he discovered he had an unlimited capacity for baseness and docility. But in only a few hours it had disappeared. He was still afraid of being dismissed from his job at the school, but since seeing Lucrecia it was as if someone else was running this risk, rising meekly every morning to take his pupils through their hymns. He rang the school. A voice — perhaps the same clerical voice that had revived in Floro Bloom a hereditary urge to desecrate convents — coldly and suspiciously wished him a speedy recovery. He didn't care. Billy Swann was still waiting for him in Copenhagen. Very soon it would be time to start a new life, his real one, the one that music had always predicted but that he only really felt when it was revealed to him by the fervour in Lucrecia's eyes. It struck him that he'd truly learnt how to play only when he started wanting her to listen to him, to desire him; that if he was ever privileged enough to attain perfection it would be out of loyalty to the future that Lucrecia forecast the first time she heard him play at the Lady Bird, when not even he thought he could ever be a real musician like Billy Swann.

'She invented me,' said Biralbo on one of the last evenings, when we no longer went to the Metropolitano. 'I wasn't as good as she thought, I didn't deserve her enthusiasm. Who knows, maybe I got better so that Lucrecia would never discover I was a fraud.'

'Nobody can invent anyone else,' I said, feeling that perhaps it was a pity. 'You'd been playing a long time before you met her. Floro always said it was Billy Swann who made you realize you were a musician.'

'Billy Swann or Lucrecia.' Lying on his hotel bed Biralbo hunched his shoulders, as if cold. 'It makes no difference. In those days I only existed if someone thought about me.'

It occurred to me that if this was true, I had never existed, but I said nothing. I asked Biralbo about his dinner with Lucrecia — where they went, what they talked about. He couldn't remember the name of the place; pain had almost erased the evening from his memory. All that remained after it was over was his loneliness, and the long taxi journey home, headlights illuminating the road ahead, silence, smoke from his cigarette, windows of solitary hillside buildings lit up in the thick fog. His life with Lucrecia had always been like this: a complicated game of escapes by taxi, nighttime journeys through the blank space of what might have been. That evening, the old feeling of failure and the emptiness in his stomach told him exactly what to expect. Alone, at home, listening to records that no longer held out the promise of happiness, he combed his hair in front of the mirror and chose a tie as though it wasn't really him who would be seeing Lucrecia, as if she hadn't really returned.

She had rented a flat opposite the station, two virtually empty rooms with a view of the dark river lined with trees, and the last bridges. At eight o'clock Biralbo was at the entrance, but couldn't quite bring himself to go in. He stood around for a while staring at the posters outside a cinema and then wandered through the gloomy cloisters of San Telmo, waiting in vain for the minutes to pass. Near by, across the street, in the darkness, the waves rose up over the handrail along the Paseo Maritimo with a gleam of phosphorus.

As he watched the waves he realized why he felt this had all happened before. He'd wandered like this in one of his dreams of cities at night. He was about to live through something that had already, mysteriously, happened in Lucrecia's absence and was now irrevocable.

At last he went up. Standing in front of an unfriendly door, he rang the bell several times before she answered. He heard her apologize for the state of the flat. He waited for a long time in a dining room containing nothing but an armchair and a typewriter, listening to the sound of the shower, examining the books lined up on the floor and against the wall. There were cardboard boxes, an ashtray full of cigarette ends, an electric heater that wasn't turned on. On top, a half-open black handbag. He imagined it was the one where she'd kept the letter she gave to Billy Swann. Lucrecia was still in the shower – he could hear water splashing against the shower curtain. Feeling slightly contemptible, Biralbo opened the handbag: tissues, a lipstick, a diary full of notes in German which Biralbo was painfully certain were the addresses of other men, a revolver, and a small wallet containing photographs. One of these showed Lucrecia in a navy blue coat, standing in front of a forest of yellow trees. A very tall man had his arms around her, his hands resting on her waist. There was also a letter – Biralbo was surprised to recognize his own handwriting – and a reproduction of a painting, carefully folded: a house, a path, and a blue mountain rising beyond the trees. Too late, he realized he could no longer hear the sound of the shower. Lucrecia was staring at him from the door, barefoot, with wet hair, wearing a knee-length robe. Her eyes and skin gleamed, and she looked thinner. Only shame diminished Biralbo's desire.

'I was looking for cigarettes,' he said, still holding the bag. Lucrecia came and took it from him, pointing to a packet beside the typewriter. She smelt of soap and cologne, of bare, damp skin beneath the blue robe.

'Malcolm used to do that,' she said. 'Go through my bag while I was in the shower. Once I waited until he was asleep and wrote you a letter, but I tore it into tiny pieces and went to bed. Do you know what he did? He got up, searched around in the waste-paper basket and on the floor, and put the letter together again piece by piece. It took him all night. It was pretty pointless – it was a ridiculous letter. Which was why I tore it up.'

'Billy Swann said you had a revolver.'

'And a reproduction of a Cézanne painting.' Lucrecia folded it and put it back in her handbag. 'Did he tell you that too?'

'Was the revolver Malcolm's?'

'I stole it from him. It was the only thing I took when I left.'

'So you *were* afraid of him.'

Lucrecia said nothing. She stared at him for a moment with tenderness and surprise, as if unaccustomed to his presence, or to the empty flat where neither of them belonged. The only lamp stood on the floor, casting their elongated shadows diagonally across the room. Lucrecia disappeared into the bedroom, taking the handbag with her. Biralbo thought he heard her lock the door. Resting his elbows on the windowsill he looked out at the river and the lights of the city. He tried to push away the incredible idea that only a few feet away, behind the locked door, Lucrecia might be sitting on the bed, perfumed, naked, putting on stockings and delicate underwear that would accentuate the pink tones of her pale skin in the dim light.

From that window the city looked completely different: shiny, dark, like the vision of Berlin that had recurred in his dreams, and enclosed by the pitch black of night and the white line of the sea. 'We dream of the same city,' Lucrecia had written in one of her last letters, 'but I call it San Sebastian and you call it Berlin.'

Now it was Lisbon. Long before she left for Berlin, ever since Biralbo had known her, Lucrecia had always believed uneasily that her true life awaited her somewhere else, among strangers, and it made her secretly reject the places she was in. Longingly, she would pronounce the names of cities where, were she ever to go, she could fulfil her destiny. For years she would have given anything to live in Prague, New York, Berlin, Vienna. Now Lisbon. She had leaflets, newspaper cuttings, a Portuguese dictionary, and a large map of Lisbon. Biralbo couldn't find the name Burma on it. 'I have to go there as soon as I can,' she told him that evening. 'It's like the end of the earth. Imagine how sailors must have felt in the past when they set off on the high seas and could no longer see land.'

'I'm going with you,' said Biralbo. 'Don't you remember? We always talked of running away together to a foreign city.'

'But you've always stayed in San Sebastian.'

'I kept my promise, I waited for you.'

'Nobody could wait so long.'

'I did.'

'I never asked you to.'

'And I never meant to. But it wasn't a question of will. These last months, I didn't think I was waiting for you any more. But I was. I'm still waiting for you now.'

'I don't want you to.'

'Tell me why you've come back then.'

'I'm just passing through. I'm on my way to Lisbon.'

I realize that in this story what happens is limited to names – Lisbon, Lucrecia, the title of that hazy song I still listen to. Names, like music, Biralbo once said with the wisdom of the third or fourth gin, take the people and places they refer to out of time, and evoke the present simply with their mysterious sound. That was how he was able to write the song without ever having been to Lisbon. The city existed before he went there, just as, even though I've never been there, it now exists for me, pink and ochre in the midday sun, misty against the gleaming sea, perfumed by the syllables of its name, as if by some dark breath – Lisbon – by the sound of Lucrecia's name. But Biralbo claimed that you have to relinquish even names, because they might contain a hidden memory, and you have to excise memory entirely if you are to go on living, to go out and walk to a café as though you were really alive.

But that was something else he learnt only after Lucrecia's return, after their slow evening of talking and drinking when he suddenly realized he'd lost everything, that he'd been robbed of the right to go on living within the memory of something that no longer existed. They drank in out-of-the-way bars, the same places they used to go to hide from Malcolm. Thanks to the gin and white wine they went back to their old game of pretence and irony, of words uttered as if not said and silence dissolved by a single glance or small coincidence, that made Lucrecia laugh grate-fully as they walked along arm in arm, like a married couple, or as she stared at him in silence, sitting in a bar. Laughter had always been their saviour – a suicidal, elegant gesture, making fun of themselves. It was a mask they shared to hide their despair, their terror, but which still left them infinitely alone, condemned and lost.

From the side of one of the twin hills that enclose the dark, quiet bay, they looked out at the city. The restaurant had candles and silver cutlery and waiters who stood motionless in the shadows, arms crossed over long, white aprons. Biralbo, who loved places when Lucrecia was there, savoured every minute with the serene avarice of someone finding himself with more treasure than he ever dared hope for. Like the city outside the windows, the night before him seemed dark, limitless, slightly bitter, not entirely propitious, but at least it was real, almost within reach, familiar and impure like Lucrecia's face. They had both changed and now had to look at each other as if for the first time, without invoking the sacred fire that distance had corrupted. They had to free themselves of nostalgia, for time had improved them and their loyalty had not been in vain. Biralbo realized that none of this could save him, that their avid recognition of each other didn't preclude the harsh truth that they were both entirely alone, but confirmed it, like some terrible axiom. He thought: 'I desire her so much I can't lose her.' And that's when he repeated that he would take her to Lisbon.

'But don't you see?' said Lucrecia quietly, her voice muted in the candlelight. 'I have to go alone.'

'Is there someone waiting for you there?'

'No. But that doesn't matter.'

'Is Burma the name of a bar?'

'Did Toussaints Morton tell you that?'

'He said you left Malcolm because you were still in love with me.'

Lucrecia looked at Biralbo through the blue-grey cigarette smoke as if from the other side of the world, but also as if she were inside him and could see herself through his eyes.

'Is the Lady Bird still open?' she asked, although perhaps it wasn't what she had intended to say.

'I thought you didn't want to go there.'

'I do now. I want to hear you play.'

'I have a piano at my flat, and a bottle of bourbon.'

'I want to hear you play at the Lady Bird. Do you think Floro Bloom's still there?'

'He must have closed up by now. But I've got a key.'

'Take me to the Lady Bird.'

'I'll take you to Lisbon. Whenever you want — tomorrow, tonight even. I'll leave my job at the school. Floro's right, they do make me take my pupils to mass.'

'Let's go to the Lady Bird. I want you to play that song, "All The Things You Are".'

A taxi dropped them off at two o'clock. The place was closed. Floro Bloom and I had left at one, having waited for Biralbo in vain. Perhaps Lucrecia had succumbed to nostalgia. She turned up her collar against the drizzle and asked Biralbo to switch on the neon sign for a few minutes. It cast flickering pinks and blues on the wet pavement, and her face, which seemed even paler. Inside, the Lady Bird smelt like a garage or a basement, and reeked of cigarette smoke. They went on playing their old game with impunity, as if on stage in an empty theatre. Biralbo switched on the lights and poured drinks. He looked at Lucrecia from the piano. As though filtered through memory, one thing followed another in a definitive and abstract way: he played and she listened, sitting at the bar, as she used to on evenings long ago. But now there was nothing and no one else there, as if in the distorted memory of a dream. Born to be fugitives they had always loved films, music, foreign cities. Lucrecia leant on the bar, sipped her whisky and said, as if making fun of herself and Biralbo and what she was about to say and loving him above all else: 'Play it again. Play it again for me.'

'Sam,' he said, for the complicity of laughter. 'Samtiago Biralbo.'

His hands were cold and he'd drunk too much – inevitably his fingers would fail to keep up with the speed of the music in his mind – but his clumsiness felt very much like fear. His hands hovered above the keyboard, seeming to emerge from the polished surface, alone and detached, as if belonging to someone else, or no one. Hesitantly he played a few notes, but didn't have time to trace the whole shape of the melody. Glass in hand, Lucrecia walked towards him, taller and slower in her high heels.

'I've always played for you,' said Biralbo. 'Even before we met. Even when you were in Berlin and I thought you'd never come back. Music means nothing to me unless you're listening.'

'It was your destiny.' Lucrecia stood on the stage by the piano, firm and distant, one step away from Biralbo. 'I've just been a pretext.'

Closing his eyes to hide from the frightening truth he'd glimpsed in Lucrecia's eyes, Biralbo played the opening bars of the song again – 'All The Things You Are' – as if the music could still protect or save him. Lucrecia moved closer and calmly placed her hand on the keyboard.

'You haven't looked at me yet,' she said. 'You've avoided looking at me.'

'I've done nothing else since you called. Before I even saw you I was imagining what you looked like.'

'I don't want you to imagine me.' Lucrecia put a cigarette between her lips. She didn't wait for him to light it for her. 'I want you to see me. Look at me. I'm not the same person I was then, who wrote you letters from Berlin.'

'I like you better now. You're more real.'

'You don't see it, do you?' Lucrecia looked at him sadly, as one looks at the sick. 'Time's passed. Not just a week or a month, but three whole years, Santiago. How many days did we spend together? Tell me.'

'You tell me why you wanted to come to the Lady Bird.'

But she didn't answer. Lucrecia turned slowly and went to the telephone, her hands deep in her coat pockets as if suddenly cold. Biralbo heard her order a taxi. Without moving, he watched her as she said goodbye from the door. As they faced each other along the length of the bar, the depth and darkness of the emptiness was like a slow blow to the face. It was an abyss he was able to measure for the first time: until that night and that conversation he hadn't even glimpsed it. He put down the lid of the piano, washed their glasses in the sink and turned out the lights. Outside, as he lowered the Lady Bird's metal shutter, he was surprised that he couldn't yet feel the pain.

'Ghosts,' said Floro Bloom, picking up the ashtray and examining it with a certain unction, as if it were a communion plate. 'Wearing lipstick.' Carrying a glass in his other hand, he went into the store room, muttering, head bowed, the skirts of his cassock rustling as he walked, as if heading for the vestry after mass. He put the ashtray and glass on the desk and rubbed his hands. 'Ghosts,' he repeated, pointing gravely at three cigarette ends stained with red lipstick. Unshaven, his cassock unbuttoned at the neck, he looked like a licentious verger. 'A female ghost. A very impatient one. Lights a lot of cigarettes and leaves them half smoked. Have you seen the film *Phantom Lady*? And two glasses in the sink. Tidy ghosts.'

'Biralbo?'

'Who else? The visitor from the shadows.' Floro Bloom emptied the ashtray and ceremoniously buttoned his cassock, savouring a swig of whisky. 'That's the problem with old bars. They're full of ghosts. You go into the toilets and there's a ghost in there washing its hands. Souls from purgatory.' He took another sip, and raised his glass to the Republican flag. 'Apparitions.'

'Maybe they're scared away when they see you in that cassock.'

'Top-quality cloth.' Floro Bloom effortlessly picked up a large box of bottles and carried it to the bar. 'From an ecclesiastical and military outfitter. Do you know how long I've had this cassock? Eighteen years. Made to measure. It was the only thing I took away from the seminary when I was expelled. Ideal as a housecoat. What's the time?'

'Eight.'

'Well, I'll have to open up then.' Floro removed the cassock, sighing sadly. 'I wonder if young Biralbo will come to play tonight.'

'Who do you think he brought here yesterday?'

'A chaste and ghostly woman.' Floro Bloom lifted a curtain and gestured towards the hard little bed he or I occasionally used. 'He didn't sleep with her. Not here at least. So that leaves only one possibility: the beautiful Lucrecia.'

'So you both knew,' said Biralbo. Like anyone who's been dominated by an obsession he was surprised that others could have any knowledge of his most intimate matter, a distant memory he was now forced to revise. 'But Floro didn't say anything at the time.'

'He was hurt. He'd say to me: "What a disloyal pair. I was their go-between when times were tough and now they hide from me."'

'*We* didn't hide.' Biralbo sounded as if the pain could still touch him. 'She did. I didn't see her either.'

'But you took that trip together.'

'I only went part of the way. I didn't get to Lisbon until much later.'

I still listen to that song. Like a story I've heard many times I know every detail, every trap the music lays for me. I hear the simultaneous voices of the trumpet and the piano, almost directing them, knowing at every moment what's coming as if I were inventing the song and the story as I listened to it, slow and oblique, like a conversation overheard behind a door, like the memory of my last winter in San Sebastian. It's true, there are cities and faces that you get to know only to lose them again: you get nothing back, neither what you once had, nor what you deserved.

'It was like suddenly waking up,' said Biralbo. 'Like when you fall asleep in the day and wake up at dusk and can't recognize the light, not knowing where or who you are. It happens to people in hospital, Billy Swann told me in that clinic in Lisbon. He woke up and thought he was dead, dreaming that he was alive and was still Billy Swann. Like that story about the sleeping saints of Ephesus that Floro Bloom liked so much, do you remember? After Lucrecia left I turned out the lights at the Lady Bird and went out into the street, and suddenly three years passed, just then, in five minutes. I could hear her voice saying it over and over as I walked home: "Three whole years." I can still hear her if I close my eyes.'

He told me that he woke with surprise from pain and solitude to a world and a time without resonance, as if from then on he would be living in a padded cell. Ever since he had known Lucrecia the city, music, his memories and his life had been interwoven with a play of coincidences and signs delicately sustaining each other, he said, like the different instruments in a jazz band. Billy Swann used to say that what mattered in music was not skill but resonance – in an empty space, a club full of noise and cigarette smoke, or in somebody's soul. Isn't it that, a pure resonance, a moment of time and prophecy, I feel when I listen to those songs – 'Burma' and 'Lisbon' – that Billy Swann and Biralbo played together?

Suddenly Biralbo saw the last few years of his life swallowed by silence, like buildings collapsing into the sea. From now on the world would no longer be a system of symbols alluding to Lucrecia. Every gesture, every desire, every song that he played would simply extinguish itself like a flame that dies without a trace. After a few days, maybe weeks, Biralbo felt entitled to call that voiceless wasteland resignation, or serenity. Pride and the habit of solitude helped: since any gesture he made would inevitably become a plea, he was not going to go after Lucrecia, or write to her, or drink in any of the bars near her flat. He arrived at school on time every morning, and at five-thirty caught the Mole home, reading the paper or staring in silence at the suburbs rushing by. He stopped playing records. All the songs he listened to – those he most loved, which he could play with his eyes shut – were now proof that he'd been cheated. When he drank a lot he composed long letters in his head, but never wrote them, and just sat staring obstinately at the telephone. He thought of an evening many years before, when he'd just met Lucrecia and was playing with the idea of sleeping with her though they'd only spoken three or four times, at the Lady Bird and the Vienna. It was very late so he was surprised by the knock at the door. When he opened it, Lucrecia was standing there, entirely unexpected, apologizing, saying she'd brought something, a book or a record she'd apparently promised to lend him and Biralbo had forgotten about.

He started involuntarily each time the phone or doorbell rang and despaired at his moral weakness in hoping it was Lucrecia. One night Floro Bloom and I went to see him. His dazed look when he opened the door showed that he'd spent many hours alone. As we walked down the passage Floro Bloom solemnly raised a bottle of Irish whiskey in both hands, and imitated the sound of a bell.

'*Hoc est enim corpus meum,*' he said as he poured the drinks. '*Hic est enim calix sanguinis mei.* Pure malt, Biralbo, just arrived from old Ireland.'

Biralbo put on a record. He said he'd been ill. With a look of relief he went to the kitchen in search of ice. He moved silently, unused to being the host, smiling half-heartedly as Floro joked and settled himself in a rocking chair, demanding drinks and cards for poker.

'We were afraid so, Biralbo,' Floro said. 'And as the bar's shut today we decided to come on a mission of mercy: to bring drink to the thirsty, set the errant on the right path, visit the sick, teach the ignorant, bestow good advice on whoever may need it . . . Are you in need of good advice, Biralbo?'

I have only a vague recollection of the rest of the evening. I was uncomfortable, became drunk immediately and lost at poker. Around midnight, with the room full of cigarette smoke, the telephone rang. Floro Bloom glanced at me out of the corner of his eye, his face flushed with whiskey. After a lot to drink his blue eyes seemed smaller and more intense. Biralbo took a while to answer the phone. For a moment all three of us stared at each other as if we'd been expecting the call.

'Let's make three tabernacles,' said Floro as Biralbo went to the phone. I felt it had been ringing for ages and was about to stop. 'One for Elias, one for Moses . . .'

'It's me,' said Biralbo, looking at us warily, not wanting us to know what he was agreeing to. 'Yes. Right now. I'll get a taxi. I'll be about fifteen minutes.'

'It's no use,' said Floro. Biralbo hung up and lit a cigarette. 'I can't remember who the third tabernacle was for . . .'

'I have to leave.' Biralbo searched for money in his pockets and put his cigarettes away, our presence of no importance. 'Stay if you want. There's beer in the fridge. I might not be back till late.'

'*Malattia d'amore* . . .' said Floro Bloom, softly so only I could hear him. Biralbo had already put on his jacket and was hurriedly combing his hair in the hall mirror. We heard him slam the door and take the lift. Barely a minute had passed since the phone call. Floro Bloom and I were now alone in Biralbo's flat, suddenly intruders in the home and life of another. 'Give shelter to the pilgrim.' Gloomily Floro held the empty bottle over his glass to get the last few drops. 'Look at him: she calls and he goes running like a little dog. Combs his hair before leaving. Abandons his closest friends . . .'

From the window I saw Biralbo leave the building and walk like a ghost fleeing through the drizzle towards where the green lights of the taxis were lined up. 'Come. Come as soon as you can,' Lucrecia had pleaded in a voice he didn't recognize, shaking with fear, or weeping, as if lost in a lethal darkness, in the distant city besieged by winter, behind one of the bright windows I could see from Biralbo's flat. Meanwhile he was again inside a dark taxi, perhaps realizing something stronger than love, that had nothing to do with tenderness but everything to do with desire and loneliness, still bound him to Lucrecia, despite themselves, against his will and his reason, against all hope.

As he got out of the taxi he saw a single light at the very top of the darkened building. Someone at the window moved away after catching sight of Biralbo standing under the streetlamp. He bounded up the interminable staircase and rang the doorbell, panting, his hands trembling. Nobody answered. After a moment he realized that the door was ajar. He pushed it open, softly calling Lucrecia's name. At the end of the passage there was a light behind a frosted glass partition. The place smelt strongly of cigar smoke and a perfume that wasn't Lucrecia's. As Biralbo entered the lit room the telephone rang out like a shot. It was on the floor, beside a typewriter, in a mess of books and papers that had been trampled by someone's very large shoes. The phone rang with cruel insistence while Biralbo looked round: the empty bedroom, still warm, the bed unmade, the bathroom, where he saw Lucrecia's blue robe, the colourless kitchen full of unwashed glasses. He returned to the dining room. For a moment he thought the telephone had stopped but jumped as it rang again, even more piercing. As he bent down to answer it he noticed that one of the papers covered in footprints was a letter he had written to Lucrecia. He heard her voice, sounding as if her hand was over the mouthpiece.

'Why did you take so long?'

'I came as soon as I could. Where are you?'

'Did anyone see you come up?'

'I thought I saw someone at the window.'

'Are you sure?'

'I think so. There are books and papers all over the floor.'

'Get out of there now. They'll be watching.'

'Tell me what's going on, Lucrecia.'

'I'm in the Parte Vieja, at the Hostal Cubana, by the Plaza de la Trinidad.'

'I'll leave now.'

'Take a roundabout route. Don't come near until you're sure no one's following.'

Biralbo was about to ask her something when she hung up. He stood for a moment listening to the dial tone. He looked at the mud-stained letter: it was dated October two years earlier. He put it in his pocket with a vague sense of loyalty to himself and turned off the light. He leant out the window and thought he saw someone hiding in a doorway, the ember of a cigarette. The headlights of a car reassured him: the doorway was empty. He closed the door quietly and descended the stairs trying not to make a sound. On the bottom landing the sound of a conversation made him stop. There was a brief snatch of music, as if someone had opened and closed a door, then a woman's laughter. Biralbo stood motionless in the dark, waiting for silence to return before continuing. Relieved but still wary, he walked towards the strip of light that came in from the streetlamp, as pale and cold as moonlight. A shadow suddenly appeared in it. Biralbo was dazed for a moment by the murky light from the doorway. In front of him, so close he could have touched it, he saw the dark, smiling face of a man with bovine eyes, and an enormous hand coming towards him with a strange slowness. As if from very far away, he heard a voice pronouncing his name – 'my dear Bigalbo.' He pushed the body away with a violence which surprised him and ran towards the door, glimpsing, as if in a flash of lightning, a head of blond hair and a hand holding a gun.

His shoulder hurt badly. He remembered the sound of a body falling heavily and an oath in French. He ran, searching for the narrow streets of the Parte Vieja. A cold salt wind struck him in the face and he realized he didn't know where he was. His footsteps echoed on the damp pavement, through the deserted streets, or perhaps they were the footsteps of his pursuer. With unaccustomed clarity, Lucrecia's face appeared in his imagination. He was losing his breath but kept running, across an illuminated square with a palace and a clock, and smelt the odour of damp earth and ferns on the Monte Urgull, feeling invulnerable and afraid that if he didn't stop running he might lose consciousness. A woman smoking in a red-lit doorway stared as he passed. He leant against a wall, gasping for breath, feeling like he'd emerged from a dark well, his eyes closed, the cold, smooth stone against his back. Opening his eyes, he was blinded by the rain, and his hair was dripping wet. He was next to the church of Santa María del Mar. The streets leading up to it were empty. Above him, above the roofs and belltowers, in the rain falling quietly through yellow and grey mist, he could hear seagulls flapping their wings. At the ends of the dark streets, the tall buildings along the boulevards shone as if illuminated by nocturnal floodlights. Trembling with cold and fear, Biralbo emerged from the darkness, walking very close to the walls and the shutters of bars now closed. He turned round from time to time, but it seemed he was the only person walking through the deserted city that night.

The Hostal Cubana was almost as filthy as the name promised. Its corridors smelt of sweaty sheets and humid walls, the stale air of the closets. Behind the desk in the lobby a hunchback pedalled on an exercise bike. He wiped the sweat from his face with a dirty towel, peering suspiciously at Biralbo.

'The young lady is expecting you,' he said. 'Room twenty-one, at the end of the corridor.'

He put on his glasses, making his eyes seem bigger, and indicated a shadowy corner. Biralbo noticed that the man's hands were swollen, almost blue, and shook slightly.

'Hey,' he called after Biralbo who was already heading down the corridor. 'Don't go thinking we generally allow this kind of thing.'

From behind the closed doors Biralbo could hear the movement of bodies and drunken snoring. Again he was gripped by a
feeling of unreality – when he knocked on the door of Room 21 he
couldn't believe that Lucrecia would really come to open it. He
knocked cautiously three times, as if it were an agreed signal.
There was no response; he thought that perhaps again he would
push open the door to find nobody there, that he was lost and
would never find Lucrecia.

He heard the sound of a bed creaking, bare feet walking on
uneven tiles, then a cough and the door being unlocked. Once
again he caught the smell of stale sweat and damp walls but he
couldn't connect that sensation with the unassailable joy of looking
into Lucrecia's grey-brown eyes after so many days. Hair loose, in
black trousers and a tight mauve T-shirt, she looked taller and
thinner. She closed the door behind her; leaning against it she
embraced Biralbo for a long time, without letting go of her
revolver. Fear or cold made her quiver, as if with desire. He glanced
round at the squalid bed, bedside table and lamp with an embroi-
dered shade, remembering with a stab of pity how she had always
loved luxury hotels. This isn't happening, he thought, we're not
here, Lucrecia isn't embracing me, she hasn't come back.

'Did they follow you?' Her face had changed. Time, or maybe
loneliness, had been cruel. If she was no longer beautiful Biralbo
didn't care.

'I ran all the way. They couldn't have caught up with me.'

'Give me a cigarette. I haven't had one since I locked myself in
here.'

'Why is Toussaints Morton after you?'

'Did you see him?'

'I pushed him over. But first I noticed his secretary's perfume.'

'*Poison*. She never uses anything else. He buys it for her.'

Lucrecia lay on the bed, still trembling, greedily drawing on the cigarette. Biralbo noticed tenderly the red marks on her feet unaccustomed to high-heeled shoes. He leant over and kissed her lightly on both cheeks. She'd had to run away, like him, and her hair was damp, her hands frozen.

She spoke very slowly, her eyes closed, at times pressing her lips together so Biralbo wouldn't hear her teeth chattering when she shivered. She gripped Biralbo's hand to her chest, digging her pale fingernails into his knuckles, as though scared he might leave or that if she let go she might drown in fear. When she trembled she lost the thread of her story, an agitation like a fever erasing her words. She sat up in bed, and put a cigarette between her lips – no longer pink but chapped and tense with obstinacy and solitude, occasionally softening into her old smile. Biralbo had almost forgotten it – it was the way she smiled when she was about to kiss him, years ago. But he realized she wasn't smiling at him – she was like a sleeping child, smiling in a dream.

For the first time she spoke of her life in Berlin: of the cold, the uncertainty, of rented rooms even more sordid than the Hostal Cubana. She talked about Malcolm, who for some reason had lost the protection of his old bosses and his job on that dubious art review nobody ever saw. She spent several months working for incomprehensible Germans, looking after their children and cleaning their houses and offices, until Malcolm came home one day with some money, all smiles and smelling of drink, announcing that their run of bad luck would soon be over. A week or two later they moved to another apartment, and Toussaints Morton and his secretary, Daphne, appeared.

'I swear to you I don't know where the money came from,' said

Lucrecia. 'I didn't care. At least I no longer had to put up with cockroaches scattering from the kitchen sink when I turned on the light. Malcolm and Toussaints acted as if they had known each other for ever, joking and roaring with laughter, and shut themselves away with his secretary to talk business, as they put it. They'd go off on week-long trips and when Malcolm got back he'd show me wads of dollars or Swiss francs and say: "I promised you, didn't I, Lucrecia? I promised you your husband would do something really big." Then Toussaints and Daphne disappeared suddenly and Malcolm became very jumpy. We had to leave the flat and we went to the north of Italy, to Milan, for a change of scenery he said . . .'

'Were the police after them?'

'We went back to the rooms with the cockroaches. Malcolm spent the days lying on the bed cursing Toussaints Morton, swearing he'd give him something to think about if he ever caught him. One day he collected a letter from the *poste restante*. He came home with a bottle of champagne and said we were going back to Berlin. That was in October last year. Toussaints Morton was his best friend once more and he forgot all the insults he'd prepared. He was pulling wads of bills out of his pockets again – he never liked banks or savings accounts. Before he went to bed he counted the money and then put it in the bedside table drawer under his gun . . .'

Lucrecia fell silent. For a few moments Biralbo listened to her uneven breathing, and then suddenly felt her chest shake beneath his hand. She bit her lip, trying to contain a convulsive shudder. She glanced at the bedside table, at the revolver gleaming in the small circle of light cast by the lamp, then looked at Biralbo distantly, gratefully, as if she were a patient and he her visitor.

'Toussaints and Daphne came to eat with us almost every day. They brought expensive wines, caviar – I assumed it was fake – smoked salmon, that sort of thing. Toussaints tied his napkin round his neck and always proposed a toast. He said we were like one big happy family . . . On Sundays, if the weather was good, we'd go out to the country. Malcolm and Toussaints loved getting up early and preparing the food. They'd load up the car with baskets, table-cloths, boxes of bottles, and by the time we left they were drunk – at least Malcolm was, I don't think Toussaints ever got drunk, despite all that talking and laughing. It seemed they were always pretending we were like those happy married couples. It was all the same to Daphne, she just smiled, but hardly ever spoke to me, she didn't trust me. She watched me, always very discreetly, with that air she had watching television and getting bored. Sometimes she even took out needles and a ball of wool and began to knit. Malcolm and Toussaints would be somewhere else, drinking, chopping firewood, playing pranks on each other, which amused them both hugely, telling dirty jokes quietly so we wouldn't hear. At Christmas they came over and said they'd rented a cabin by a lake, in the forest. They suggested we spend New Year's Eve there – an intimate party, only a few guests. In the end just one turned up. They called him the Portuguese, but he looked more like a Belgian or a German, very tall, with tattoos on his arms and always drunk on beer. When he finished a can he'd crush it in his hand and throw it anywhere. I remember one day – the morning of the thirty-first – he'd been drinking as usual and went up to Daphne, I think he touched her, and she took one of her needles and held it to his neck; he went still and very pale, then left the room and didn't look at Daphne or me for the rest of the day, until later that night, when Toussaints was strangling him, on the sofa where he used to stretch out to drink his beer. I can still remember how his eyes bulged, and his face went purple and blue, and his hands . . . Malcolm had told me that they were going to pull off the biggest deal of their lives with the Portuguese; we'd be able to retire to the Riviera on all the money they were going to make, something to do with a painting. The three of them spent the morning walking by the lake, even though it was snowing heavily, and I could see them stop from time to time and gesticulate, as if they were arguing. They came back and shut themselves in another room while Daphne and I made lunch and they were shouting but I couldn't make out what they were saying because Daphne had turned up the volume on the radio. They came out much later, the food had gone cold, and they were very quiet, all three looking very serious, Toussaints glancing at Daphne from time to time out of the corner of his eye, smiling and making signs to her, and looking at Malcolm without saying anything while the Portuguese ate very noisily, not speaking, in a T-shirt despite the cold. He looked like he'd been an athlete or something before becoming an alcoholic, those tattoos which covered his arms made me think he had been a legionnaire in Indochina or Africa, and his skin was deeply tanned. Outside it was still snowing and night was falling, with a strange new silence, and I felt something was going to happen; my face was burning – I'd drunk a lot of wine – so I put on my jacket and went out, walking through the forest for a while, towards the lake, when suddenly I seemed to be a long way away, almost lost, and I couldn't go forwards because I kept sinking into the snow and my feet were getting frozen. It was dark by then as I went back to the cabin, guiding myself by the light from a window, and when I got there I saw what they were doing to the Portuguese. He was right in front of me, looking at me through the window, but the silence made everything seem far away, like a lie or one of those games Toussaints was so fond of, as if they were pretending to strangle someone. But it was real. The Portuguese's face was blue and his eyes were staring at me as Toussaints stood behind him, leaning over his shoulder, like he was whispering in his ear, and Malcolm had the man's arm twisted behind his back and held a gun to his chest, digging it into the white T-shirt while the veins stood out on the Portuguese's neck, circled by something very thin and shiny, a nylon cord which I'd seen Toussaints playing with before, twisting it in his fingers, like the long toothpick he used to clean his nails . . . I could see Daphne there too, but her back was to me, as still as when she knitted or watched television. The Portuguese was kicking weakly – I remember he was wearing jeans and army boots – then I couldn't hear him kicking the floorboards any more, and the snow got in my eyes. Toussaints and Malcolm saw me. I didn't move. Daphne turned around too and the Portuguese's eyes were still fixed on me, but he couldn't see me any more, his legs shook a bit and then stopped moving and Malcolm took the gun away from his chest and the Portuguese was still staring at me . . .'

She didn't run away: when Malcolm came out to look for her, she stood trembling, immobile, stupefied by the cold. She recalled what happened then as if she had watched it through a frosted window. Malcolm pushed her gently inside the cabin and took off her wet jacket. Then she was sitting on the sofa with a glass of brandy in front of her, and Malcolm was treating her with the vile attentiveness of a guilty husband.

She watched them impassively. Toussaints came back from the garage brushing snow from his shoulders and carrying a rough piece of canvas and a rope, and knelt in front of the Portuguese, talking to him as if he were a patient who hadn't yet come round from the anaesthetic. He stretched out the man's legs while Malcolm lifted his shoulders and Daphne spread the canvas on the floor, at Lucrecia's feet. The body thumped back heavily, the huge gnarled hands on its stomach, the tattooed arms, the head at a strange angle, the eyes closed now Toussaints had passed his hand over the lids. They moved around the corpse like brisk, efficient nurses, wrapping it in the canvas. Malcolm raised the head to wind the rope round the neck, and let it fall back sharply. They bound the feet, the waist, wrapping the canvas tightly round the body, now just a heavy, shapeless bundle that made them pant and curse as they lifted it and carried it out, bumping into doorways and corners of furniture, led by Daphne wearing gumboots and a pink raincoat, and holding in her right hand a carbide lamp, which, outside on the road leading to the lake, made the snowflakes glow in a night as dark as a windowless cellar. From the cabin door, Lucrecia watched them disappear into the darkness, feeling confused and weak, as if she'd lost a lot of blood. Their voices reached her, muffled by the snow – Toussaints's curses, Malcolm's nasal, jerky English. She could even hear the sound of their breathing, and then the blows of an axe, because the lake was frozen over, and finally a splash, like a large rock being thrown in. Then silence. The wind scattered the sound of their voices through the trees.

The following morning they went back to town. The surface of the lake had frozen over again, smooth, immutable. For several days Lucrecia felt dead, in a drug-induced sleep. Malcolm looked after her, brought her presents and huge bunches of flowers. He spoke softly, and never mentioned Toussaints Morton or Daphne, who had disappeared. He said they'd move to a bigger flat very soon. As soon as she could get up, Lucrecia fled. Now, almost a year later, she was still fleeing, she couldn't imagine that she would ever stop.

'And meanwhile I was here,' said Biralbo, overcome by guilt, by the banality of turning up for classes every morning, placidly accepting postponement, the suspicion of failure, waiting like a lovesick teenager for letters that never came. Far from Lucrecia, he waited pointlessly, meekly bearing the pain, ignorant of real life and its cruelty. He leant towards her and stroked the sharp cheek-bones that seemed to rise out of the darkness like those of a drowned woman. He felt tears and, as his fingers brushed her chin, a slight tremor that spread to her entire body, like the ripples from a stone dropped into water. Her eyes shut, Lucrecia pulled him towards her, embraced him, grasping his waist and thighs, digging her nails into the back of his neck, as rigid with cold and fear as she had been the night when her breath misted the window as a man was slowly strangled. 'You made me a promise,' she said, her face buried in Biralbo's chest. She raised herself on her elbows to hold his stomach within the hard edges of her hips and reach up to his mouth, as if afraid of losing him. 'Take me to Lisbon.'

He drove, excited by fear and speed. This wasn't like before, surrendering to taxi journeys, or slumping in front of a bottle of bourbon, or being carried on a train hurtling into the night. Now he controlled the force of time, like when he played the piano, when the band and the audience were propelled into the future, into the void, by his daring imagination and the dizzying speed and discipline of his hands moving over the keyboard; he was like a jockey both tightening the reins and digging his heels into the horse's side — he didn't tame the music or restrain its spirit, but it surrendered to him. Now, driving Floro Bloom's car, he was calm, a man finally operating at the limits of his potential, at the most advanced level of his life. He had left behind the mirages created by his memory and his resignation, and savoured the feeling of remaining warm and still while moving at a hundred kilometres an hour. He was grateful for every second that took them further and further away from San Sebastian, as if the distance detached them from the past and protected them from its curse – protected only him and Lucrecia, fugitives from a doomed city now invisible behind the hills and the mist so that neither of them gave in to the temptation to look back. The trembling needle lit up on the dashboard did not measure their speed but this boldness of soul, the windscreen wipers methodically swept aside the rain to show the road to Lisbon. Lucrecia's face was reflected in the windscreen. He'd turn slightly to look at her when she placed a lit cigarette between his lips, and watch out of the corner of his eye as she tuned the radio, or turned up the volume of a song on one of the tapes they found in the car. Perhaps Floro had left them there deliberately – recordings made at the Lady Bird in the old days, when Biralbo played with Billy Swann and she went up to him afterwards and said she'd never heard anyone play the piano like that. I'd like to think they listened to the recording made the evening that Malcolm introduced me to Lucrecia, and that among the background noise of clinking glasses and conversation, with Billy Swann's trumpet rising keenly above it, there was a faint trace of my voice.

They listened to music as they headed west along the coast road, the cliffs and the sea always to their right. They had recognized the secret hymns that bound them together even before they met because later, when they listened to them together, they would see the songs as part of the symmetry of their previous lives, signs that fate had arranged everything so they should meet, even the music of certain ballads from the thirties. 'Fly me to the moon,' Lucrecia said as they left behind the last streets of San Sebastian. 'Take me to the moon, to Lisbon.'

Around six, as it was getting dark, they stopped at a motel. Set well back from the road, only the light from the windows was visible through the trees. As he locked the car Biralbo heard the rumble of low tide nearby. Lucrecia was waiting for him in the light of the lobby, her travel bag on her shoulder and her hands in the pockets of a long checked coat. Biralbo's normal sense of time faded again; when he was with her he had to measure it differently. The previous night, the visit from Floro Bloom and me, everything before Lucrecia called him belonged to the distant past. He had been driving for five or six hours, but in his memory they were as insubstantial as a few minutes: he couldn't believe only that morning he'd been in San Sebastian, or that the town still existed, so far away, in the darkness.

But we did still exist. I enjoy simultaneous occurrences: so, maybe, while Biralbo was checking in at the motel, Floro Bloom and I were talking about him. Floro was buttoning his cassock, looking at me sadly, as if he'd been unable to avert a disaster.

'He turned up at my place at eight this morning. Who would have thought of doing that, with the hangover I had? I nearly fainted when I got up, and went to the door cursing in Latin. He kept ringing the bell, like an alarm clock that wouldn't stop. I opened the door: Biralbo. With eyes this big, as though he hadn't slept, and that dark shadow he gets when he doesn't shave. At first I couldn't understand what he was saying. I asked him, "Maestro, did you sit up all night praying while we were asleep?" But he didn't take any notice, he didn't have time for jokes. He made me splash my face with cold water and didn't even let me make coffee. He wanted me to go to his flat and gave me a list of the things to bring back – his ID, chequebook, some clean shirts, that kind of thing. Ah, and a packet of letters in the drawer by his bed. From guess who. Then he got all cagey – as if I was in a fit state to deal with that kind of thing, at that time of the morning. "Floro, don't ask me any questions, I can't tell you anything." I was already outside when he came after me: he'd forgotten to give me the keys. When I got back he greeted me like I was a messenger from the Tsar. He'd drunk about a pint of coffee and looked like he was smoking two cigarettes at once. He had one last favour to ask. "Isn't that what friends are for?" I said. "Taking advantage of you and not telling you a thing." He wanted to borrow my car. I asked where he was going, and he went all mysterious again, "I'll tell you as soon as I can." I gave him the keys and told him to write, but he didn't hear me, he'd already left . . .'

They were given a room without a view of the sea, big but not very welcoming or propitious, its luxury marred by hints of past adulteries. As they walked to the room Biralbo felt that his fragile happiness was slipping away, that he was afraid. To overcome his fear he thought, 'What I've always wanted has happened to me: I'm at a hotel with Lucrecia and she won't be leaving in an hour's time, when I wake up tomorrow morning she'll be here with me, and we'll go to Lisbon.' He locked the door behind them, and turned to kiss her, feeling for her slim waist beneath the coat. There was too much light; Lucrecia left just the bedside lamp on. They behaved with vague courtesy, slightly cold, as if trying to avoid the fact that they were going to sleep together for the first time in three years.

They found a fridge full of drinks hidden under an austere dressing table. Like guests at a party full of strangers, they sat next to each other on the bed with their drinks between their knees. Every movement was like an intimation of something that didn't happen. Lucrecia lay back on the pillow, staring at her glass, the ice cubes edged with gold by the light, silently looking at Biralbo, and in her eyes, veiled by tiredness and disbelief, he recognized the fervour of the past. She'd lost her innocence, but he didn't care, he preferred her like this – wiser, rescued from her fear, vulnerable and as mesmerizing as the statue of a goddess. No one could find them there, at a motel in the middle of nowhere, surrounded by the night and the storm beating against the windows; he had the revolver now and would know how to protect her. He was leaning cautiously towards her when she started, as if a noise had woken her from sleep, and looked out of the window. They heard a car engine, and the sound of tyres on the gravel drive.

'They can't have followed us,' said Biralbo. 'This isn't the main road.'

'They followed me to San Sebastian.' Lucrecia leant out the window. There was another car beside theirs outside the motel, among the trees.

'Wait here.' Checking the safety catch on the revolver, Biralbo left the room. He wasn't afraid, but worried that fear might turn Lucrecia back into a stranger.

In the lobby a travelling salesman was joking with the receptionist. The two men fell silent when they saw Biralbo; no doubt they'd been discussing women. Biralbo put the revolver in the glove compartment and drove to a nearby restaurant where a neon sign offered snacks and sandwiches. On his way back, the lights of a petrol station appeared remarkable, endowed with the symbolic quality of those first images when arriving at night in an unknown country – isolated stations, dark towns with shuttered houses. He parked among the trees, hearing the damp bracken crunching beneath the tyres. Walking towards the motel he looked up – Lucrecia was waiting for him behind one of those windows.

Without regret he thought of everything he'd left behind: San Sebastian, his old life, his teaching job, the Lady Bird, where Floro would have switched on the lights by now.

As he came into the lobby the receptionist whispered to the salesman and they both stared at him. He asked for his key. He thought the salesman was slightly drunk. The receptionist, a thin, very pale man, smiled broadly as he handed over the key and wished him a good night. Biralbo heard stifled laughter as he went towards the lift. He didn't dare admit to himself his anxiety; he needed one of those spectacular glasses of bourbon that Floro Bloom kept in a secret cupboard at the Lady Bird for his closest friends. As he put the key in the lock he thought, 'One day I'll see that my whole life was summed up in this gesture.'

'Provisions for a siege,' he said, showing Lucrecia the bag of sandwiches. He hadn't looked at her yet. She was sitting up in bed, knees bent, wearing a bra and covered to the waist by the sheet. She was reading one of the letters she wrote from Berlin. Empty envelopes and handwritten pages were spread out around her bent knees and over the bedside table. She gathered them up, jumped lightly from the bed and went in search of beer and paper cups. A flimsy dark garment that shone like silk covered her pubis and drew a delicate line across her hips. Her hair, straight and fragrant, swung about her face. She opened two cans of beer, foam spilling over her hands, and put the sandwiches and cups on a tray. She seemed not to sense Biralbo's stillness, his desire. She sipped her beer and smiled, pushing her hair off her face.

'It's so strange reading these old letters.'

'Why did you want me to bring them?'

'To find out what I was like then.'

'But you never told me the truth in them.'

'What I wrote in those letters was the only truth. My real life was a lie. I saved myself by writing them.'

'It was me you were saving. I lived for your letters. When they no longer came I stopped existing.'

'What lives we've had.' Lucrecia folded her arms across her chest, as though she was cold or hugging herself. 'Writing letters or waiting for them, living on words, for so long, so far away from each other.'

'You were always with me, even though I couldn't see you. As I walked along the street I told you what I saw. If I heard a song on the radio that moved me I thought, "I'm sure Lucrecia would like this." But I don't want to think about any of that. We're here now. You were right, the other night at the Lady Bird: memories deceive, we're not reliving what happened three years ago.'

'I'm frightened.' Lucrecia picked up a cigarette and waited for him to light it for her. 'Maybe it's too late.'

'We've survived so much. We're not going to lose each other now.'

'Maybe we already have.'

He knew that gesture Lucrecia made with the corners of her mouth, that look of pity and resignation that time had left in her eyes. But he realized that it was no longer a brief sign of dismay, as in the past, but a permanent habit of her soul.

Involuntarily, step by step, they were performing a ceremony of commemoration. As on their first night, more indelible in his mind than this one, Lucrecia turned out the light before slipping between the sheets. Now too he finished his cigarette and his drink in the dark. Clumsy, fumbling, he undressed, in a vain attempt at discretion that continued during his first caresses. He hadn't been able to remember certain things: the taste of Lucrecia's mouth, her long, delicate thighs, the swell of joy and desire as they became entwined with his.

But he told me that a part of his mind remained lucid, wary and alone, untouched by the fever, by the kisses, as if he were still sitting in the dark, cigarette glowing, watching himself embrace Lucrecia, whispering to himself that it wasn't really happening, he wasn't recovering his long-lost fulfilment, but was trying — eyes closed and body blindly clinging to Lucrecia's cold thighs — to recreate and hold on to a particular night, unrepeatable, imaginary, forgotten.

He noticed the mutual rancour of the kisses, the solitary nature of his desire, the relief granted by darkness. He searched her for the mildly hostile proximity of another body, not yet willing to accept what his hands perceived, the obstinate stillness, that wariness of one who has repudiated the fire. He kept hearing that voice whispering in his ear, he saw himself again standing in a corner of the room, an indifferent spy, smoking and observing the useless noise of the bodies, the anxiety of the two shadows who breathed as if raking the ground.

Afterwards he turned on the light and searched for cigarettes. Without lifting her head from the pillow Lucrecia asked him to switch the light off. Before he did, Biralbo saw the shine of her eyes behind untidy hair. Walking lightly in bare feet, she went to the bathroom. The sound of the taps being turned on and water swirling down the drain struck Biralbo's ears like an insult. She came out, leaving the light shining as weakly as inside a refrigerator. He watched her come towards him, naked, bending over slightly. She got into bed, shivering, and wrapped herself round him, chin trembling, her face still damp. But such signs of tenderness no longer filled Biralbo with hope. He was certain now that she was different, and had been since her return, perhaps before she had even left. It wasn't distance that had deceived them, but the temerity of thinking they could triumph over it, the pretence of talking, lighting cigarettes, as if they didn't know by then that anything they said was futile.

Later, Biralbo didn't remember whether he managed to sleep. He knew that he held her for many hours in the room lit only by a slant of light from the bathroom, and that his desire never diminished. At times, still asleep, Lucrecia caressed him and smiled and said things he couldn't understand. She had a nightmare and woke trembling, he had to grip her hands to stop her from digging her nails into his face. She turned on the light as though to make sure she was really awake. The overheated room made it difficult to sleep, and Biralbo hovered on the blurred edges of dreams; he could still see the room, the window, the furniture, even their clothes on the floor, but he was back in San Sebastian, or Lucrecia wasn't with him, or it was some other woman he held so tightly.

He knew he had fallen asleep when he woke with a start, certain someone was moving about the room – a woman, with her back to him, wearing a strange red robe: Lucrecia. He watched her carefully open the fridge and pour herself a drink. He didn't want her to know he was awake so he closed his eyes when she leant over the bedside table for a cigarette. The lighter flame lit up her face. She sat down by the window as if preparing to wait for dawn. Putting her glass on the floor she leant forward – she seemed to be trying to make something out through the window.

'You're no good at pretending,' she said as he came up behind her. 'I knew you weren't asleep.'

'You're not much good at it either.'

'Would you rather I was?'

'I knew immediately. The first time I touched you. But I didn't want to find out for sure.'

'I felt we weren't alone. When you turned out the light all I could see were faces: the people who must have slept here before us; and yours — not now but as it was three years ago; and Malcolm's, when he was on top of me and I didn't refuse.'

'So Malcolm is still watching us.'

'He felt very close, in the room next door, listening. I dreamed about him.'

'You tried to scratch my face.'

'When I saw it was you I was all right. The bad dreams stopped.'

'But you woke up again.'

'I hardly ever sleep now. In Geneva, if I ever got any money, I bought Valium and cigarettes first, and food with what was left over.'

'You didn't tell me you lived in Geneva.'

'For three months, after leaving Berlin. I starved. In Geneva, not having money is worse than being a dog or a cockroach. And I saw hundreds of those, all over the place. I wrote you letters and then threw them away. I looked at myself in the mirror and wondered what you'd think if you could see me. You can't imagine what you look like when you have to go to bed hungry. I was scared I might die in one of those rooms or in the street and be buried without anyone knowing who I was.'

'Is that where you met the man in the photograph?'

'Who?'

'The man with his arms around you in the forest.'

'I haven't forgiven you for searching my handbag.'

'I know: that's what Malcolm used to do. Who was he?'

'You're jealous.'

'Yes. Did you sleep with him?'

'He ran a photocopying business. He gave me a job. I almost fainted on his doorstep.'

'You were sleeping with him.'

'What does it matter?'

'It matters to me. You didn't see faces in the dark when you were with him?'

'You don't understand anything. I was alone. I was running away from people who were trying to kill me. There was goodness in him, something neither you nor I have. He was kind and generous and never asked questions, even when he saw your photo in my wallet – that newspaper cutting you sent me. And he didn't say anything when I asked him to pay for the clinic. He acted as if he believed he was responsible.'

Lucrecia waited in silence for a question that never came. Her mouth was dry and her lungs hurt but she kept smoking with a passion alien to pleasure. Beyond the trees, dawn was breaking in a smooth, grey sky in which night still lingered, streaked with purple. They hadn't heard the sea for hours now. Soon first light would raise the mist among the trees. She stood at the window, not looking at Biralbo. She went on talking, maybe not so that he would know or share, but so that he would receive his part of the punishment, his exact dose of indignity and shame.

'That night in the cabin. I didn't tell you everything. They gave me brandy and sleeping pills; I could barely stand by the time Malcolm took me to bed. When I looked at him I saw the Portuguese's head on his shoulders, with his eyes open and his purple tongue hanging out of his mouth. Malcolm undressed me as if I was a child, and Toussaints and Daphne came in, smiling, like parents saying goodnight. Or maybe that happened before. Toussaints always came up very close when he spoke to me, I could smell his breath. He said, "If the good little girl doesn't keep quiet Daddy Toussaints is going to cut out her tongue." He said it in Spanish, and it sounded very strange – for months I'd been talking and even dreaming in German or English. Even you spoke to me in German when you appeared in my dreams. Then they left. I was alone with Malcolm. I could see him moving about the room, even though I was asleep. He undressed and I knew what he was going to do but couldn't stop him – it was like being chased in a dream, unable to run away. He was heavy over me, moaning, his eyes closed. He bit my mouth and my neck, and I just wanted it all to end so I could go to sleep, but he kept moving. He moaned as if he was dying, with his mouth open – he covered my face in saliva. When he finally stopped he felt as heavy as a corpse. And then I realized: he was as heavy as the Portuguese when they picked him up by his arms and legs and dropped him on to the canvas. Later, in Geneva, I had fainting fits and vomited when I stood up, but not from hunger, and I remembered Malcolm and that night. And the saliva, and the way he moaned against my mouth.'

Dawn had broken. Biralbo dressed and said he would go for coffee. When he returned Lucrecia was still staring out of the window, but now the light sharpened her features and made her skin look even paler against the red silk of the large robe she had wrapped around herself, tied at the waist and vaguely Chinese or medieval. He thought bitterly that the man in the photograph must have bought it for her. When Lucrecia sat on the bed to drink her coffee the robe parted to reveal her thighs. He had never

desired her so much. He knew he had to leave by himself, and he
had to tell her so before she asked him.

'I'll take you to Lisbon,' he said. 'I won't ask questions. I love
you.'

'You're going back to San Sebastian. You'll give Floro Bloom
back his car. Tell him I haven't forgotten him.'

'I don't care about anyone but you. I won't ask for anything, not
even that you be my lover.'

'Go with Billy Swann, get on a plane tomorrow morning. You're
going to be the best black pianist in the world.'

'It won't mean anything unless you're with me. I'll do whatever
you want. I'll make you fall in love with me again.'

'You still don't understand, do you? I'd give anything for that to
happen, but the only thing I really want is to die. Always, now,
here.'

Biralbo had never seen her look at him so tenderly, not even
when they first met. He thought with sadness and pride and
despair that no one would ever look at him like that again. As she
got up, Lucrecia kissed him, parting her lips. She let the red robe
slip to the ground and entered the bathroom naked.

Biralbo went to stand by the closed door. His hand on the door-
knob, he listened to the water running, then he put on his jacket
and took the keys. After a moment he picked up the revolver,
having pictured Toussaints Morton's smiling face. His wallet was
bulging – he remembered that before leaving San Sebastian he'd
cleaned out his bank account. He kept a few notes and left the rest
on the bedside table, between the pages of a book. He'd already
opened the door silently when he turned back: he'd forgotten
Lucrecia's letters. The sun shone yellow and horizontal through the
windows in the lobby. He could smell damp earth and thick

bracken as he walked to the car. Only when he started the engine and accepted that he was leaving for good did he understand Lucrecia's last words and her calmness as she said them. Now he too wanted to die, with the cold, vengeful intensity with which you wish for something that is yours alone, that you know you have always deserved.

At exactly midnight in the Metropolitano, the lights and the sounds of conversation faded and a red and blue glow surrounded the stage. Looking coolly efficient and experienced, like gangsters preparing to execute a crime, the members of the Giacomo Dolphin Trio sat at one end of the bar finishing their drinks and cigarettes and exchanging secret signals. Only the blonde waitress and I approached them. The double-bass player walked with the dignity and grace of a young black woman. Smiling nonchalantly he sat down on his stool, leaning the neck of the double bass against his left shoulder, and looked out at the audience as if he knew of no higher virtue than condescension. Buby, the drummer, took his place with the practised, economical movements of a wrestler sleepwalking, not hitting the drums but brushing them with circular sweeps, as if just pretending to play. He never drank alcohol and always had a glass of orange juice within reach. 'Buby's a puritan,' Biralbo told me once. 'He takes only heroin.' Biralbo himself was the last to leave the bar and his glass of whisky. With his curly hair, dark glasses and sloping shoulders, hands twitching at his sides like a gunman's, he walked slowly to the piano, staring straight ahead, and abruptly sat down on the stool, embracing the keyboard with his outstretched fingers. The room fell silent. I could hear him clicking his fingers rhythmically and tapping his foot on the floor and then, without warning, the music started, as if it had already been playing a while and we were only now allowed to hear it. There was no prelude, no initial emphasis, no beginning or end; it was like coming out into the street or opening the window on a winter's night and suddenly hearing the sound of rain.

I was mesmerized by their fixed stares and the rapid movement of their hands, of those parts of their bodies that could visibly express rhythm — head, shoulders, heels, everything moving with the instinctively synchronized movement of the gills and fins of fish in an aquarium. They seemed less to play the music than be possessed by it, imbued with it, propelling the notes towards our ears and hearts on waves of air with serene contempt born of wisdom not even they controlled, which beat unceasing and dispassionate within the music, like a pulse, or like fear and desire throbbing in the darkness. On top of the piano, beside his glass of whisky, Biralbo kept a scrap of paper on which, at the last minute, he would write the list of songs they'd play. In time I recognized them all, and knew when to expect the calm violence with which they broke up the melody, only to return to it, like a river coming back to its course after a flood. As I listened, the songs explained my life, even my memories, all the things I had ever vainly wished for, that would never be mine, and that I recognized in the music as clearly as my own face in a mirror.

Their playing built gleaming translucent structures that collapsed like breaking glass, or created long stretches of calm very close to silence but which grew imperceptibly in turbulence until your ears stung with the deliberately cruel, dissonant tangle of notes. The band smiled, eyes half closed, as if feigning innocence, as the music became as soothing as a whisper. There was always a moment of astounded silence before the applause.

Standing at the bar of the Metropolitano I stared at Biralbo — inscrutable behind dark glasses, alone, cynical, happy. Watching his elegance, unchanging and without province, I wondered if the songs were still about Lucrecia: 'Burma', 'Fly Me to the Moon', 'Just One of Those Things', 'Alabama Song', 'Lisbon'. I thought all I had to do was repeat their names and I'd understand everything. That's why it's taken me so long to comprehend what he said to me one evening: the greatest perversion a musician can commit while playing is autobiography. I had to remember, among other things, that he wasn't called Santiago Biralbo now, but Giacomo Dolphin — he'd asked me always to call him that in front of others. It wasn't just a ruse to elude the police; for over a year it had been his only true name, the sign he had decisively broken the spell of the past.

Between San Sebastian and Madrid his biography was a blank space crossed only by the name of a single city, Lisbon, and the dates and places of a few recordings. He left San Sebastian without saying goodbye to either Floro Bloom or me, even on the last night we spent drinking at the Lady Bird, disappearing as cautiously and resolutely as though he was leaving for ever. He lived in Copenhagen for a while, where he made his first record with Billy Swann; it doesn't include either 'Burma' or 'Lisbon'. Sometime in the middle of '84 after touring Germany and Sweden, the Billy Swann Quartet – including someone not yet named Giacomo Dolphin – played various clubs in New York. After that, I know from magazine advertisements I saw in Biralbo's papers that in the summer the Giacomo Dolphin Trio played several clubs in Quebec. (When I read this, I remembered Floro Bloom and the squirrels eating from his hand; it gave me a lasting feeling of gratitude and exile.) In September 1984 Billy Swann missed an Italian festival because he'd been admitted to a clinic in France. Two months later a magazine denied rumours of his death, saying he was about to give a concert in Lisbon. Santiago Biralbo wasn't playing with him; according to the newspapers, the pianist accompanying Billy Swann on the evening of 12 December in a concert hall in Lisbon was a musician of Irish or Italian origin called Giacomo Dolphin.

At the beginning of that month Biralbo had been in Paris, doing nothing in particular, not even walking around the city, which bored him. He lay on his hotel bed reading crime novels, drank till late in smoke-filled clubs and didn't talk to anybody because he could never be bothered with French – he told me he tired quickly of speaking it, the way you do of drinking very sweet liqueurs. So he was in Paris but could have been anywhere, alone, waiting vaguely for a contract that never came, but not really caring about that either, even hoping that they'd take weeks to call him, so when the telephone eventually did ring it was like an unwelcome alarm call. It was Oscar, Billy Swann's double-bass player who later played with Biralbo at the Metropolitano. He was calling from Lisbon, his voice sounding very distant, and Biralbo took a moment to understand what he was saying: Billy Swann was very ill, the doctors thought he was going to die. Oscar said he'd started drinking again – he drank himself unconscious and then carried on drinking when he came to. One day he'd collapsed in a bar and had to be taken by ambulance to one of those clinics for drunks and lunatics, an old sanatorium that looked like a castle on a wooded hillside outside Lisbon. He was drifting in and out of consciousness and calling Biralbo's name or talking to him as if he were by the bed, not so he could be told anything but so he would come as soon as possible to play with him. 'Though it's not likely he'll ever play again,' said Oscar. Biralbo wrote down the address of the hospital and hung up. He packed some clean clothes, his passport, the crime novels – the belongings of a drifter. He was going to Lisbon, but didn't yet connect the name of the city where Billy Swann might die with the title of a song he'd written, a place that had long been sealed in his memory. Only when he saw the word 'Lisbon' in luminous letters on the departures board a few hours later at the airport, did he remember what the name had meant to him, long ago, in another life. He realized that all the towns he'd lived in since leaving San Sebastian were stages of a journey that might now be about to end. He'd been waiting and running away for so long, but in two hours' time, he'd be in Lisbon.

He'd pictured a city as misty as San Sebastian or Paris and was surprised by the transparency of the air, the precise pink and ochre of the façades, the red roofs, the static golden light that hung over the hills as if it had just rained. He took a room in a hotel with dark corridors where everyone seemed to whisper. From his window he could see a square with many identical balconies, and the profile of a statue of a king on horseback pointing emphatically south. He found that Portuguese spoken quickly was as incomprehensible as Swedish. They understood his Spanish, however — he was told that the place he wanted was very near Lisbon. At a vast, ancient station he caught a train which immediately entered a long tunnel; when it emerged it was already getting dark. He saw districts of tall buildings in which lights already burnt, and almost deserted stations where dark-skinned men stared at the train as though they had been waiting a long time but then didn't get on. Occasionally there was a burst of light at his window, from a train heading back to Lisbon. Unsettled by the solitude and silence he stared at unknown faces and unfamiliar surroundings as if they were the yellow sparks that appear in the dark when you close your eyes. Yet if he closed his eyes he was no longer in Lisbon: he was in the Paris Métro, or on a train crossing birch forests in northern Europe.

The train grew emptier at every stop. When he was alone in the carriage Biralbo feared he'd missed his station. He sat, anxious and disheartened, like a passenger on the deserted underground late at night, worried he's on the wrong train or that there's no driver. At last he got off at a dirty station with tiled walls. There was a woman walking along the platform with a torch, reminding Biralbo of the large underwater flashlights divers once used, who told him how to get to the sanatorium. It was a humid, moonless night, and as he came out of the station Biralbo noticed a strong smell of damp earth and pine trees. It was exactly the same on certain winter nights in San Sebastian, on the thickly wooded Monte Urgull.

He walked along the poorly lit road, and beneath the fear that Billy Swann might already have died lay the feeling that he was in danger, stirring memories within him. It made everything seem symbolic – the lights of the isolated houses, the smell of the forest at night, the sound of water dripping and running somewhere near by, among the trees. The station was now out of sight, and the road and the darkness seemed to close in on him. He was worried he might not have understood the woman's directions, but then, as he came round a bend, he saw the huge dark shape of a mountain dotted with lights, and a village huddled round a palace or castle with tall columns and arches and strange conical towers or chimneys lit from below, magnified in what seemed like torch-light.

It was just like being lost in the landscape of a dream, walking towards the sole light that flickers in the darkness. Then, to his left, he found the road the woman mentioned, and a sign for the sanatorium. The way wound uphill through the trees, dimly lit by low, yellow lights almost hidden in the undergrowth. He thought of something Lucrecia once said: arriving in Lisbon would be like reaching the end of the earth. He suddenly remembered that he'd dreamt about her the night before – a short, bitter dream in which he saw her face, unfamiliar as when they first met many years earlier, with such precision that he only recognized her when he woke up. He thought it must be the smell of the forest that made him think of her. Breaking his habit of forgetting, he let his memory take him back to San Sebastian, and then to another more distant place he couldn't yet identify, like coming into a station whose name he couldn't make out from the train. It seemed, he explained to me in Madrid, that since arriving in Lisbon the boundaries of time, his commitment to the present and to forgetting – the result of discipline and will-power, like his wisdom in music – were gradually dissolving; as if at some point on the road through the forest he had crossed an invisible frontier between two enemy countries. Approaching the hospital entrance and with lights in the hall and cars parked outside, he realized he hadn't been remembering a walk through San Sebastian near the slopes of the Monte Urgull; it wasn't the smell or the feeling of damp and mist that revived his grief over losing Lucrecia at a dif-ferent stage of his life. He was remembering another place, another night, the lights of a hotel, the gleam of a car hidden

among pines and bracken, a journey to Lisbon cut short – the last
time he was with her.

A nun in a wimple which spread like white wings around her
head told him that visiting hours were over. He explained he'd
come a great distance to see Billy Swann, that he was afraid Billy
Swann might die if he left it another day or even another hour.
Head down, the nun smiled for the first time. She was young and
had blue eyes and spoke quietly in English. 'Mr Swann isn't going
to die. Not for the time being.' Going ahead of him, taking very
small steps, she led Biralbo along cold, tiled corridors to Billy
Swann's room, her stiff white wimple bobbing. From the high
arched ceilings hung dusty globes of light, like in old cinemas, and
at every landing and bend in the corridor doormen in grey uniforms sat dozing at desks which looked like they'd been salvaged
from old offices. Oscar, the double-bass player, was slumped on a
bench facing a closed door, his powerful arms crossed, his head on
his chest, as if he'd only just fallen asleep.

'He hasn't moved since they brought Mr Swann in,' the nun
whispered.

Oscar sat up, rubbing his eyes, and smiled at Biralbo with surprise and weary gratitude.

'He's recovered,' he said. 'He's much better today. He was worried he'd missed the concert.'

'When are you supposed to be playing?'

'Next week. He's convinced we'll make it.'

'Mr Swann is out of his mind.' The nun shook her head, her
wimple flapping.

'You'll play,' said Biralbo. 'Billy Swann's immortal.'

'Difficult.' Oscar was still rubbing his eyes with his large, white-
tipped fingers. 'The pianist and the drummer have left.'

'I'll play with you.'

'The old man was offended you didn't come to Lisbon,' said Oscar. 'When we first brought him here, he didn't want us to let you know. But while he was delirious he called out your name.'

'You can go in now,' said the nun from the door. 'Mr Swann is awake.'

Even before seeing him and smelling the odour of sickness and medicine, Biralbo was seized by deep feelings of loyalty and tenderness. But he also felt guilt and pity, and relief, because he had refused to go to Lisbon with Billy Swann and as punishment he'd almost never seen him again. What a cheap betrayal, I once heard Biralbo say, to put love before friendship even when you're no longer in love. He went into the room but it was so dark he couldn't see Billy Swann. There was a large window and a plastic sofa, on which lay the trumpet case, and on the right a high white bed and a lamp casting its diagonal light over Billy Swann's hard, simian features, his frail body in absurd striped pyjamas barely visible beneath the covers. Arms straight by his sides and head resting on several pillows, Billy Swann lay as motionless as though posing for a statue. When he heard voices he opened his eyes and felt for his glasses on the bedside table.

'Son of a bitch,' he said, pointing a finger with a long, yellow nail at Oscar. 'I told you not to call him. I said I didn't want to see him in Lisbon. You thought I was going to die, didn't you? So you asked all the old gang to Billy Swann's funeral.'

His hands trembled slightly, more emaciated than ever, just skin on bone, like his cheeks and forehead and tensed, corpse-like jaws. His body was reduced to bones, a parody of the living man it once supported, just a ribcage and skin, criss-crossed by the veins of an alcoholic. His black glasses seemed to form part of his skeleton, of what would remain of him long after he was dead. But in his eyes and the bitter line of his mouth, pride and mockery survived intact as if set into a horrible mask, together with his ineffable right to blaspheme and disapprove, stronger than ever now that he was looking death in the face with the same contempt with which he once looked at failure.

'So you came,' he said to Biralbo, leaning on him like a crafty boxer in a clinch when Biralbo put his arms around him. 'You wouldn't play with me in Lisbon, but you came to see me die.'

'I've come to ask for a job, Billy,' said Biralbo. 'Oscar tells me you don't have a piano player.'

'Judas.' Keeping his glasses on, Billy Swann laid his head back on the pillows. 'No, I don't have a drummer or a piano player. Nobody wants to play with a dead man. What were you up to in Paris?'

'Lying around reading novels. You're not dead, Billy. You're more alive than any of us.'

'Tell that to Oscar and the nun and the doctor. They lean over the bed and peer at me as if I was already lying in my coffin.'

'We'll play together on the twelfth, Billy. Like in Copenhagen, in the old days.'

'What do you know about the old days, boy? They were over long before you were born. The others died just in time – for the last thirty years they've been playing in hell, or wherever it is God sends people like us. Look at me, I'm a shadow, an exile. Not from my country, but from that era. Those of us left pretend we're still alive, but we're lying, we're frauds.'

'You never lie when you play.'

'No, but I don't tell the truth either.'

Billy Swann burst out laughing, his face contracting as if in a spasm of pain. Biralbo pictured him as he looked on his early

record covers, a roguish lock of hair slicked down over his forehead. With the years Billy Swann's face had shrunk: his forehead,
still bearing a vestige of that bold lock, had shrivelled, while his
nose, mouth and cleft chin – which almost disappeared when he
played the trumpet – were drawn into a grimace that reminded
Biralbo of a shrunken head. Biralbo thought maybe he was dead
after all, but that no one had ever managed to crush him. No one,
and nothing, not even drink or obscurity.

There was a knock at the door and Oscar, standing like a silent
guard, opened it a little to see who it was. The nun's bobbing,
winged head appeared. She looked round the room as if searching
for a secret stash of whisky. She said it was very late, they ought to
let Billy Swann get some sleep.

'I never sleep, sister,' said Billy Swann. 'Bring me a bottle of con-
secrated wine, or ask your Catholic God to cure my insomnia.'

'I'll come back tomorrow,' said Biralbo, who hadn't lost a child-
ish fear of nuns' white habits and was prepared to obey her
immediately. 'Call me if you need anything. Whatever the time.
Oscar has the number of my hotel.'

'I don't want you to come back,' said Billy Swann, his eyes magnified by his glasses. 'Leave Lisbon, tomorrow morning, or tonight.
And take Oscar with you. I don't want you here waiting for me to die.'

'We'll play together on the twelfth, Billy.'

'You didn't want to come to Lisbon, remember?' Billy Swann sat
up, with Oscar's help, not looking at Biralbo, as if he were blind. 'I
know you were scared of coming here. That's why you lied about
playing in Paris. Don't change your mind now. You're still scared.
Do what I say: leave and don't look back.'

But that night it was Billy Swann who was afraid, Biralbo said,
afraid of dying or of somebody watching him die, of not being

alone during his final hours. He was afraid not just for himself, but for Biralbo, perhaps only for Biralbo. Billy Swann didn't want him seeing something that he himself had glimpsed in that hospital room at the end of the earth. He told Biralbo to leave, as if trying to get him off a sinking ship, to prevent him being touched by death. He fell back against the pillows. The nun pulled the sheet up under his chin and turned out the light.

When Biralbo reached the station he was surprised to discover it was only nine o'clock. The hospital, the forest, the village and the castle with its conical towers and ivy-clad walls looked as if they existed only at night, never touched by dawn, that they must dissolve like mist with the sun. In the station canteen he drank an opal-coloured *eau-de-vie* and smoked a cigarette while waiting for his train. Excited, and a little afraid, he felt alien here, more than in Stockholm or Paris, because at least those cities appeared on maps. With the fearsome independence of someone alone in a strange country, he had another drink and got on the train, knowing exactly the state of mind he would be in from the alcohol, the journey, the solitude. On seeing the city lights, he said 'Lisbon', like it was the name of a woman for whom he felt nothing. In a station that looked abandoned, the train stopped alongside another heading in the opposite direction. The whistle blew and both trains moved off slowly, with the sound of clashing metal. Looking through the windows of the other train, Biralbo saw faces he would never see again, distant yet distinct, staring back in a reflection of his melancholy. In the last carriage, just before the red lights and darkness, a woman sat smoking, head bowed, so lost in her own thoughts that she didn't look up when her train set off. She had very short hair and wore a navy blue coat with the collar turned up. 'It was the hair,'

Biralbo told me later. 'That's why I didn't recognize her at first.' He stood up and waved, in vain – his train was already speeding through a tunnel by the time he realized that in that instant he had seen Lucrecia.

He couldn't remember for how long, how many hours or days, he wandered in a trance through the worst of Lisbon's neighbourhoods, down dirty alleys, up steps to scenic vantage points, through colonnaded squares with statues of kings on horseback, among the huge sombre warehouses and rubbish dumps of the port, across an endless red bridge over a river as vast as the sea, through suburbs with blocks of flats rising from open ground like lighthouses or islands, past ghostly train stations on the outskirts of the city, trying in vain to remember the name of the one where he saw Lucrecia. He was trying to outwit fate, to make the impossible repeat itself: one by one, he looked at the face of every woman he saw, passing him in the street, or sitting by the window in trams or buses, in the back of a taxi, or leaning out of a window in a deserted street. Old, expressionless, ordinary, brazen faces;

countless gestures and expressions and blue coats that never belonged to Lucrecia, as interchangeable as the crossroads, the dark hallways, the red roofs and maze of streets in the poor quarters of Lisbon. A weary tenacity that in the past he would have called desperation swept him on, like a swimmer without the strength to fight the current. Even when he allowed himself to rest in a café, he chose a table looking on to the street. And from the taxi returning to his hotel at night he searched the deserted avenues and street corners lit by neon signs where women stood and waited, arms crossed. When he switched off the light and lay on the bed smoking, he could still see faces and streets and crowds flashing before his half-closed eyes, like images from a magic lantern. He was so tired he couldn't sleep; as if his eyes, desperate to go on searching, had abandoned the exhausted body lying on the bed and gone out into the city, losing themselves there until the night was over.

He was no longer sure that he had seen Lucrecia, or that it was love driving him to search for her. In the daze of those who wander alone through unfamiliar cities, he didn't know whether he was looking for her, only that he couldn't find peace, at any time of the day or night, that every one of the narrow streets climbing Lisbon's steep hills or dropping as abruptly as ravines drew him on, secretly, relentlessly. Perhaps he should have left while he still could, when Billy Swann told him to, but it was too late, as though he'd missed the last train out of a besieged city.

In the mornings he went to the sanatorium. In vain he watched the windows of the passing trains, and read the names of the stations until he knew them by heart. Wrapped in a huge dressing gown with a blanket over his knees, Billy Swann spent his days staring at the forest and the village from his window. He

hardly ever spoke. Without turning he would simply lift his hand
to ask for a cigarette, but then let it burn down after one or two
drags. Biralbo looked at his back against the grey light at the
window, as still and solitary as a statue in an empty square.
Smoke rose from the cigarette held in his long, curved hand. A
slight movement would knock the ash on to the floor beside
him without his seeming to realize; coming closer one noticed
the slight, ceaseless trembling of his hand. A warm mist, wet
from the rain, enveloped the landscape and made everything
seem distant. Biralbo thought he'd never seen Billy Swann so
meek and calm, so detached from everything, even music and
alcohol. From time to time, he would sing – a few verses from a
love song or an old Negro spiritual – very quietly, sweetly, in his
thin cracked voice, always with his back to the room, facing the
window, and then pucker his lips and lazily imitate the sound of
a trumpet. The first morning that Biralbo went to visit him, he
heard him improvising strange variations on a tune both
unknown and familiar: 'Lisbon'. Biralbo hesitated by the half-
open door; Billy Swann didn't seem to have heard him and was
humming as if alone, tapping his foot gently.

'So you didn't leave,' he said, without turning round, staring at
the window as though Biralbo was reflected there.

'I saw Lucrecia last night.'

'Who?' Billy Swann turned now. He had shaved, and his hair,
thinning but still black, shone with brilliantine. In his glasses and
dressing gown he looked like a placid little old man. But that was
quickly belied by the fire in his eyes and the strange tautness of the
skin over his cheekbones. Biralbo thought the cheeks of a freshly
shaven corpse must shine that way.

'Lucrecia. Don't try to tell me you can't remember her.'

'The girl I saw in Berlin,' said Billy Swann, in a tone between sorrow and mockery. 'Are you sure it wasn't a ghost? That's what I always thought she was.'

'I saw her on a train heading this way.'

'Are you asking if she's been to see me?'

'It had crossed my mind.'

'Only you and Oscar would think of coming to a place like this. The corridors smell of death. Haven't you noticed? Disinfectant, chloroform, and flowers, like a New York funeral parlour. At night you can hear screaming – guys strapped to their beds imagining cockroaches climbing up their legs.'

'It was only for a moment.' Biralbo now stood beside Billy Swann and stared at the dark misty forest, the houses dotted along the valley, smoke rising from their chimneys, the railway sheds in the distance. A train was entering the station silently. 'It took me a minute to recognize her. She's cut her hair.'

'It was your imagination, boy. This is a very strange country. Things are different here, as if they happened years ago and you're just remembering them.'

'She was on that train, Billy, I'm sure of it.'

'What difference does it make?' Billy Swann slowly took off his glasses, as he always did when he wanted to convey the full force of his contempt. 'I thought you were cured. We made a deal, remember? I'd stop drinking and you'd stop picking at old wounds.'

'You didn't stop drinking.'

'I have now. Billy Swann will go to his grave as sober as a Mormon.'

'Have you seen Lucrecia?'

Billy Swann put his glasses back on but didn't look at him. He was staring at the rain-darkened towers of the castle when he spoke

again, with a studied and neutral intonation, as if addressing a servant, or someone one doesn't see.

'Ask Oscar if you don't believe me. He won't lie to you. Ask him
if a ghost has been to visit me.'

'I was the ghost, not Lucrecia,' Biralbo said to me the last night
we spent together, more than a year later as he lay on the bed of
his hotel room in Madrid. He was shamelessly, quietly drunk on
whisky, lucid and oblivious to everything, as if talking to a mirror.
He was the one who had almost ceased to exist; it was he who,
wandering all over Lisbon, was gradually fading away, like the
memory of a face seen just once. Oscar also denied that a woman
had been to visit Billy Swann – he was sure of it, he was always
there, he would have seen her, why would he lie? Again Biralbo
took the road through the forest and had a drink at the station
while waiting for the train back to Lisbon. He stared out at the
pink plaster walls and white arches of the sanatorium, and thought
of Billy Swann sitting, strangely still, at one of the windows.
Biralbo could almost feel him watching with disapproval, and he
remembered him quietly singing the song Biralbo wrote long
before coming to Lisbon.

He went back to abandon himself to the city, as though to
one of those endless nights of music and bourbon. Winter had
cast its shadow over the streets and gulls flew over the roofs and
statues of horsemen, in search of a refuge from the storms at sea.
Every evening, as night fell, there was a moment when it became
clear that the sky wished for winter. Mist rose from the river,
obscuring the horizon and the tallest buildings on the hills, and
the red bridge stretched over the grey waters into a void. But
then lights came on – lines of streetlamps along the avenues,
signs flickering on and off, fleeting lines of neon tracing a name

or picture, rhythmically colouring the low Lisbon sky pink and red and blue.

Sleepless, he kept walking, collar turned up, recognizing places he'd passed many times, then realizing he was lost just when he had been most sure he'd learnt the pattern of the city. It was, he told me, like drinking a fragrant gin as transparent as glass or a cold December morning, like injecting yourself with a sweet poisonous substance that expanded your mind beyond the limits of reason or fear. He perceived everything with an icy precision, sometimes glimpsing how easy it would be to slide into madness. He learnt that anything might become the first sign of an hallucination for someone alone for a long time in a foreign city; the face of the waiter serving him coffee or the receptionist to whom he handed his key were as unreal as the Lucrecia he'd found and just as suddenly lost again, or his own face in the bathroom mirror.

He never stopped searching for her, and almost never thought about her. Just as the mist and waters of the Tagus cut Lisbon off from the rest of the world, transforming the city from a place into a landscape of time, he discovered for the first time in his life the absolute isolation of his acts: his own past and future were becoming as alien to him as the objects that surrounded him at night in his hotel room. Perhaps it was in Lisbon he first experienced the brave and self-contained happiness I saw the first night I heard him play at the Metropolitano. I remember him once saying that Lisbon was the home of his soul, the only possible home for those who are born foreigners. And for those who choose to live and die like renegades: one of Billy Swann's axioms was that any man of decency ends up hating his country and leaving for good, shaking the dust from his sandals.

One afternoon, lost and weary, Biralbo found himself in a suburb too remote to walk back from before nightfall. Abandoned red brick warehouses bordered the river. On the rubbish-strewn banks old machines lay among the weeds, looking like skeletons of extinct animals. Biralbo heard a familiar sound in the distance, like the scraping of metal. A tram approached, tall and yellow, swaying on its rails, making its way slowly between blackened walls and slag heaps. Biralbo got on. He couldn't understand what the driver said, but didn't care where the tram was going. In the distance, over the city, the winter sun glowed, shrouded in mist, but the landscape Biralbo crossed was as grey as a rainy afternoon. After a journey that seemed endless the tram stopped in a square that opened on to the estuary. It was lined with deep porticoes topped with statues and marble pediments. A flight of steps led down to the water. A statue stood on a pedestal surrounded by white elephants and angels raising bronze trumpets – a king, whose name Biralbo never discovered, holding the reins of his steed, a proud hero facing the sea wind laden with rain and the smells of the port.

Although it wasn't yet dark, lights were coming on in the high, damp gloom of the colonnades. Biralbo walked under an archway decorated with shields and allegorical figures, and was immediately lost in strange streets. In Lisbon he could never distinguish between places he'd never visited and places he'd simply forgotten. These streets were dark and narrow, lined with vast warehouses and dense with smells from the port. He walked across a square large and icy as a marble sarcophagus, with shining tram rails curving across it, and down a street edged by one long ochre wall with barred windows and no doors. He turned down a tunnel-like alley that smelt of damp basements and coffee sacks. Hearing footsteps behind him he walked faster.

He took another turning, afraid he was being followed. He gave a coin to a beggar sitting on a step with his artificial leg beside him. The leg looked dignified, orange, with a checked sock and lone shoe, all shiny, almost melancholy. He saw fishermen's taverns and doorways to boarding houses or brothels. The air was thickening, as if he were going down a well. He saw more bars and more faces – dark masks, cold almond eyes with blue eyelids, pale expressionless features staring out from pink-lit hallways, mouths like wounds holding cigarettes, calling to him from street corners, from the doors of clubs with purple velvet curtains, beneath flashing neon signs, lit despite the daylight, announcing the arrival of night.

Names of cities or countries, faraway lands, ports, films, names that glowed, mysterious and inviting, like the lights of a city seen from a plane at night, clustered together like coral or ice crystals. *Texas*, he read, *Hamburg*, words in red and blue, yellow, pale violet, slender lines of neon, *Asia*, *Jakarta*, *Mogambo*, *Goa*, all the bars and women offered themselves to him. He walked on as though tracing the journey with his finger on maps in his memory and imagination, dogged by the old sense of fear and perdition those names had always conjured in him. A black man in dark glasses and a tight raincoat spoke to him in English, holding out something in the pale palm of his hand. Biralbo shook his head but the man went on with his list: gold, heroin, a revolver. Aware of his fear, he took pleasure in it, like someone driving too fast through the night, giddy with the speed. He thought of how in an unknown city Billy Swann always went off alone to find the most dangerous streets. And then he saw it – the word in blue lights, on the last street corner, flickering as if about to go out, high up in the darkness like a lighthouse, like the lights on the last bridge in San

Sebastian. It disappeared for a moment, then flickered again, and at last the letters came on, one by one above the street, until they formed a word, calling him: *Burma*.

He went in, as though closing his eyes and leaping into a void. Blonde women with large thighs and hard, ugly faces sat drinking at the bar. The men were indistinct, standing, sitting on couches, counting coins surreptitiously, waiting outside booths with red lights above the doors. When a light went out someone would emerge from one of the cabins, head down, and another man would go in, locking the door behind him. A woman approached Biralbo. 'Just four twenty-five-escudo coins,' she said. He asked her in hesitant Portuguese why the place was called Burma. She smiled blankly, gesturing towards the line of booths. Biralbo entered one of them. It was as narrow as a train toilet and at one end there was a round window, like a porthole with opaque glass. One by one he inserted the coins in a vertical slot. The light in the cabin went out and the window was lit by a reddish glow. 'This isn't me,' thought Biralbo. 'I'm not in Lisbon, this place isn't called Burma.' Through the window a pale, almost naked woman was dancing on a revolving platform. She would pretend to caress herself, and then kneel or lie down automatically, contemptuously, writhing, occasionally glancing with dull eyes at the row of round windows.

The window of Biralbo's cabin went opaque, as if suddenly covered with frost. He emerged, feeling cold, and turned the wrong way. The tunnel of identical cabins didn't lead back to the bar, but to a bare room lit by a single bulb and with a half-open metal door. The walls were covered in damp patches and obscene drawings. Biralbo heard footsteps on metal stairs, but didn't have time to hide. A man and a woman appeared at the door, their arms around each other's waist. The man's hair was ruffled and he avoided Biralbo's gaze. Once they had disappeared, Biralbo headed down the stairs, which led to a dimly lit garage or store room. A huge luminous clock hung from metal beams above a space as empty as a deserted dance floor.

Like a railway station with gothic arches and tall smoke-blackened windows, the place gave the impression of infinite space, emphasized by the gloom, the red light bulbs above the doors, and obsessive, violent music. Behind a long empty bar a pale barman in a dinner jacket prepared a tray of drinks. Biralbo thought he had a slight dusting of pink powder on his cheeks, but perhaps it was the reddish light in the room. A bell rang and a red light came on above one of the metal doors. Holding the tray in one hand, the barman crossed the width of the room and knocked on the door. As it opened the red light went out. Through the music Biralbo thought he heard laughter and clinking glasses.

A man emerged from a door at the far end of the room, doing up his trousers with a certain brisk satisfaction, as if leaving the urinals. There was another bar there, distant, illuminated like a chapel in the depths of a cathedral. A second barman in a dinner jacket and a solitary customer stood out as distinctly as silhouettes cut from black cardboard. The man who'd zipped up his trousers pulled a hat down over his eyes and lit a cigarette. A woman followed him, fluffing up her blond hair, putting a powder compact away in her bag and pursing her lips. From the bar nearest the exit Biralbo watched them as they passed, talking quietly in a Portuguese full of sibilants and obscure vowels. The woman's heels clicked on the metal stairs outside but he could still smell her cheap, heady perfume.

'Are you alone, sir?' The barman had returned with the empty tray and was staring at him dourly from behind the marble bar. He had a very long face, hair slicked down over his forehead. 'No need to be alone here at the Burma.'

'Thanks,' said Biralbo. 'I'm waiting for someone.'

The barman smiled with lips that were too red. He obviously didn't believe Biralbo, wanting perhaps to encourage him. Biralbo ordered a gin and stood staring at the twin bar at the other end of the room. The same waiter, the same forties-style dinner jacket, the same patron, shoulders drooping, hands immobile either side of his glass. He noticed almost with relief that the other man wasn't smoking, otherwise he could have been looking into a mirror.

'Are you waiting for a woman?' The barman's Spanish was careless but efficient. 'When she arrives you can use number twenty-five. You ring the bell and I'll bring your drinks.'

'I like this place. And its name,' said Biralbo, smiling like a loyal, solitary drunk. It worried him to think that the other man was probably saying the same to the barman at the other end of the room. But the main virtue of chilled, neat gin is that it goes straight to your head. 'Why is it called Burma?'

'Are you a journalist, sir?' The barman now looked wary. His smile was frosty.

'I'm writing a book.' Biralbo felt joyfully that in lying he wasn't hiding his life, but inventing it. '*Lisbon by Night.*'

'You don't have to put everything in, do you? My bosses wouldn't like it.'

'I wasn't intending to. Just clues, you know what I mean . . . People arrive in a city and can't find what they're looking for.'

'Would you like another gin, sir?'

'You read my mind.' After so many silent days Biralbo felt a shameful desire for conversation, for lies. 'Burma. So has it been open long?'

'Almost a year. It used to be a coffee warehouse.'

'I suppose the owners went bankrupt. Was it already called Burma?'

'It wasn't called anything before, sir. Apparently they weren't really dealing in coffee. The police arrived and surrounded the whole area. Led them away in handcuffs. The case was in the newspapers.'

'So they were dealing in contraband?'

'They were up to something.' The barman leant on the bar, his face very close to Biralbo's, and whispered theatrically, 'Something political. Burma was a secret society. They kept arms here . . .'

A bell rang. The barman headed towards a door where the red light had come on, crossing the room as if taking small dance steps. The other drinker slowly detached himself from the bar at the far end and walked to the exit in a suspiciously straight line. Stripes of light and shade succeeded each other across his face. He was very tall and definitely drunk, his hands sunk in the pockets of a military-style jacket. He wasn't Portuguese, or Spanish; he didn't even look European. He had a slightly flattened face, with large teeth and a trimmed, reddish beard. The peculiar curve of his forehead was vaguely reptilian. He stopped in front of Biralbo, swaying in his large, buckled boots, smiling stupidly, with slow drunken jubilation. Looking into the man's blue eyes, Biralbo was taken back to the Lady Bird, long ago, to his open, almost adolescent joy at being loved by Lucrecia. 'Don't you remember me?' the man asked, and Biralbo recognized the laugh, the lazy, nasal voice. 'Your old buddy, Bruce Malcolm?'

'So there we were,' said Biralbo, 'face to face, staring at each other with suspicion and sympathy, like two acquaintances who were never close and realize after about five minutes they don't know what to say to each other. But he was friendly. All those years of hate and it turned out that I enjoyed talking to him about the old days. Maybe it was the gin. My heart skipped a beat when I saw him. He remembered San Sebastian, Floro Bloom, everything, and I said to myself nothing brings two men closer together than having loved the same woman. And lost her. He had lost Lucrecia too . . .'

'You talked about her?'

'I think so. After three or four gins. He looked round the bar and said, "I bet Lucrecia would like this place."'

But it had taken a long time for them to mention her, coming close but stopping before saying her name, as if they stood before a gap they pretended not to see, hiding behind words and alcohol, questions and lies about their recent lives and recollections of a past in which the most important days were indistinguishable. The blank space they took so long to dare name bound them together like an ancient pact. They ordered more drinks ('*la penúltima copa*', the one before last, said Malcolm, who still remembered some Spanish jokes) and went back further in time, competing to remember small details rescued from oblivion, with pointless precision, about how they met, Billy Swann's first gig at the Lady Bird, Floro Bloom's dry martinis (pure alchemy, according to Malcolm), coffee and cream at the Vienna – the peaceful life in San Sebastian. They couldn't believe it was only four years ago. What had they done since then? Nothing – slide into decline and sordid middle age, try to outwit misfortune, survive by selling a few pictures or playing the piano in cities where the weather was too cold. '*Soledad*. Loneliness,' said Malcolm, misty-eyed, gripping his glass as if he wanted to shatter it. Then Biralbo felt scared and cold and queasy, as if he had the beginnings of a hangover. He thought Malcolm might have a gun, the one Lucrecia saw, the one he once dug into the chest of a man who was being slowly strangled with a nylon cord . . . But no, who could believe such a story: murderers only existed in novels or news reports, they didn't sit drinking with you in a Lisbon basement, asking after mutual friends. He and Malcolm were both lonely, and drunk, and overcome with the same cowardice and nostalgia. Even in the only visible difference between them – that Malcolm wasn't smoking – they found a kind of complicity, remembering the nicotine sweets Malcolm always handed round to everyone, even Biralbo, who one night, full of bitterness and jealousy, had ground one underfoot outside the Lady

Bird. Malcolm was suddenly silent. He raised his eyes from his empty glass, looking at Biralbo without lifting his head.

'I always envied you,' he said, sounding quite different, as if he'd only pretended to be drunk up till then. 'I was sick with envy when you played the piano. We all applauded when you finished, and you'd come over to our table smiling, a drink in your hand, a look of contempt on your face, not noticing anyone.'

'It was fear. Everything scared me – playing the piano, even looking at the audience. I was afraid they'd make fun of me.'

'I envied the way women looked at you.' Malcolm went on, ignoring him. 'You couldn't care less. You didn't even see them.'

'I never believed they were looking at me,' said Biralbo. He thought Malcolm was lying, talking about someone else.

'Even Lucrecia. Her too.' Malcolm paused, as if about to reveal a secret. He drank some gin, then wiped his mouth with his hand. 'I haven't forgotten how she looked at you. You'd go up on stage, play a few notes and then nothing but your music existed for her. I remember thinking once, "That's exactly how a man wants the woman he loves to look at him." She left me, you know. All those years together and she dumps me in Berlin.'

'He's lying,' thought Biralbo, struggling against an invisible trap and the delirium of drink. 'He's pretending not to know what was going on to discover something. He's always lied – he doesn't know how not to. It's all lies – the nostalgia, the friendship, the sadness, even the shine in those eyes, too blue and cold, even if he is lost and alone in Lisbon like me, thinking of Lucrecia and talking to me just because I knew her too.' He ought to be on his guard and stop drinking, say he was leaving, get out of there as soon as possible. But his head felt heavy, the music and lights were bewildering; he'd wait a few minutes, just time for one more drink . . .

'There's something I've always wanted to ask you,' said Malcolm. He was so serious he looked sober, with the gravity of someone about to pass out. 'Something personal.' Biralbo stiffened, regretting that he'd had so much to drink and hadn't left. 'You don't have to answer. But if you do, promise that you'll tell me the truth.'

'I promise,' said Biralbo. Bracing himself, he thought, 'Now he's going to say it. Now he's going to ask me if I slept with his wife.'

'Were you in love with Lucrecia?'

'It doesn't matter now. It was a long time ago, Malcolm.'

'You promised me the truth.'

'You said I didn't notice women, not even her.'

'You noticed Lucrecia. We'd go for breakfast at the Vienna and there you would be. And at the Lady Bird. Remember? After your set you'd sit at our table, you two always talking together so you could look into each other's eyes. You both knew about books and films, you knew the names of all the actors and musicians, remember? I'd listen and always feel you were speaking a language I couldn't understand. That's why she left me. Because of the films and books and songs. Don't deny it, you were in love with her. Do you know why I took her away from San Sebastian? I'll tell you. After all, you're right, it doesn't matter any more. I took her away so she wouldn't fall in love with you. I'd have been jealous even if you'd never met. And I'll tell you something else: I'm still jealous.'

Biralbo was vaguely aware of other people in the huge basement of the Burma. Blonde women and men hidden behind the smoke of their cigarettes came and went, up and down the metal stairs; red lights above closed doors went on and off. He made his way across the immense room to the lavatory as though walking through a desert. His face very close to the cold tiles, it seemed a long time since he left Malcolm at the bar, and that it would take even longer to get back. He tried to leave but couldn't open the door, confused by the silence and the row of white ceramic urinals, multiplied in the fluorescent glare. Leaning over a basin as big as a baptismal font, he splashed his face with water. When he opened his eyes there was someone else in the mirror. Suddenly all the faces from his memory were coming back to him, as though summoned by the gin or by Lisbon, faces he thought he'd forgotten, that he thought irretrievably lost. Why flee cities if they pursue you to the ends of the earth? He was in Lisbon, in the surreal lavatory of the Burma, but the face staring at him over his shoulder – he stopped turning at the sight of the pistol – belonged to the past, to the Lady Bird: smiling with inextinguishable happiness, Toussaints Morton was pointing a gun at him. He still sounded like a film-Negro or a bad actor doing a French accent on stage. His hair was greyer and he'd put on weight, but he still wore the same shirts and gold bracelets, and oozed the same reptilian charm.

'My friend,' he said. 'Please don't put up your hands. It's vulgar. I can't stand it, even in movies. Just hold them away from your body. That's right. Allow me to search your pockets. Can you feel something cold against the back of your neck? It's my gun. Nothing in your jacket. Perfect. That just leaves your trouser pockets. I know. Don't look at me like that. This is as unpleasant for me as it is for you. Can you imagine if somebody came in now? They'd think the worst, wouldn't they, seeing me up against you in the toilets. But don't worry, our friend Malcolm is watching the door. He doesn't deserve our trust, of course. No, not yours either. And I have to confess that I didn't risk leaving him alone. I'm sure some mishap would occur if I did. So my sweet Daphne is with him. You remember Daphne, don't you? My secretary. She is looking forward to seeing you again. Nothing in your trousers. What about your socks? Some people keep a knife there. Not you. Daphne used to say, "Toussaints, Santiago Biralbo is an excellent young man. I'm not surprised Lucrecia left that brute Malcolm for him." Turn around slowly – we're going out now. Please don't think of shouting. Or running away, like the last time we met. Would you believe I'm still in pain from that blow? Daphne was right, I fell awkwardly. You may think the barman will phone the police if you call out. But you're wrong, my friend. No one will hear you. Have you noticed how many shops sell hearing aids in this town? Open the door. Please, after you. That's right, keep your hands away from your body, look straight ahead, smile. Your hair's a little untidy, you look pale. Could it be the gin? That's what you get for drinking with Malcolm. Smile at Daphne. She thinks highly of you, you know. In a straight line, please. Do you see that light over there?'

He didn't feel frightened, just ill, contrite at having had so much to drink, and with a stubborn certainty that these things didn't happen in real life. Behind him, Toussaints Morton chatted jovially with Malcolm and Daphne, his right hand in the pocket of his brown jacket, arm slightly bent, in the stiff pose of a tango dancer. As they passed beneath the large clock hanging from the ceiling their faces and hands glowed pale green. Biralbo looked up and read the motto around the clockface: *Um Oriente ao oriente do Oriente.*

Toussaints Morton quietly ordered him to stop outside one of the closed, metal doors, painted black or very dark blue like the walls and wooden floor. Head bowed meekly, Malcolm opened the door and stood aside like a bellboy to let them pass .

The room was small and narrow, and smelt of cheap soap and stale sweat. It contained a sofa, a lamp, a plastic plant and a bidet. The pink light seemed to dilute the frivolous atmospheric music of organ and guitars. 'Maybe they're going to kill me here,' Biralbo thought indifferently, disappointed, looking round at the wall-paper, the salmon-coloured upholstery of the sofa covered in long stains and cigarette burns. The four of them could barely move in the space as confined as a crowded train compartment. He could feel the gun, hard and cold, digging into his spine, and Toussaints Morton breathing heavily on the back of his neck. Daphne exam-ined the sofa harshly and sat on the edge, her knees close together. She swung her platinum-blond hair out of her face and then sat motionless, her profile to Biralbo, staring at the pink bidet.

'You sit down too,' ordered Malcolm. He was holding the gun now.

'My friend,' said Toussaints Morton, 'you'll have to excuse Malcolm's rudeness – he's had too much to drink. It's not entirely his fault. He saw you and called me; I asked him to keep you enter-tained for a while, although not to this degree, of course. Would you permit me to tell you that you too have gin on your breath?'

'It's late,' said Malcolm. 'We haven't got all night.'

'I detest this music.' Toussaints Morton peered into the corners of the room, searching for the invisible loudspeakers now weakly playing a baroque fugue. 'Turn it off, Daphne.'

Everything seemed even stranger in silence. The music outside didn't penetrate the padded walls. Toussaints Morton took a tran-sistor radio from the breast pocket of his jacket and extended the aerial until it touched the ceiling. Whistling noises mixed with voices speaking Portuguese, Italian, Spanish. He cursed and tried to tune the transistor with his huge fingers, smiling when he found something that sounded like the overture to an opera. 'He's going to hit me now,' thought Biralbo, incurable addict of the cinema. 'He'll turn the music up very loud so no one can hear me cry out.'

'I adore Rossini,' said Toussaints Morton. 'The perfect antidote to all that Verdi and Wagner.'

He placed the radio between the taps of the bidet and sat down on the edge, humming along to the music. Malcolm shifted from one foot to the other uneasily, perhaps feeling guilty, or depressed by the alcohol, pointing the gun at Biralbo and trying not to look him straight in the eye.

'My dear friend. My very dear friend.' Toussaints Morton's face broke into a broad, fatherly smile. 'This is all very unpleasant. For us too, believe me. So the sooner we do what we have to, the better. I ask you three questions, you answer any one of them and we all forget about the past. Number one, where is the fair Lucrecia? Number two, where is the picture? And number three, if the picture is no longer around, where is the money? Please, don't look at me like that, and don't say what you're about to say. You're a gentleman. I knew it the first time I saw you. You assume you have to lie to us, believing you're protecting Lucrecia, that a gentleman doesn't betray a lady's secrets. Please allow me to suggest that we're familiar with that game. We played it some time ago, in San Sebastian, if you remember.'

'I haven't heard from Lucrecia in years.' Biralbo was getting bored, as if filling in an official questionnaire.

'Strange then that you left her flat in San Sebastian one night. And were rather impolite on your way out.' Toussaints Morton touched his left shoulder as if it still hurt. 'And the next day you set off on a long journey together . . .'

'Is that true?' Malcolm seemed to wake up. He lifted the gun higher and, for the first time since they entered the room, looked straight at Biralbo. Daphne's eyes opened wide, and flicked from one side to the other, like a bird's.

'Malcolm,' said Toussaints Morton, 'I'd prefer it if after all these years you didn't choose this precise moment to realize you're the last to know. Calm down. Listen to Rossini. *La gazza ladra*.

Malcolm swore in English and held the gun slightly closer to Biralbo's head. They stared at each other in silence as if alone in the room. But rather than hatred, there was astonishment, fear, even curiosity in Malcolm's eyes.

'That's why she left me,' he said. But he wasn't talking to Biralbo, he was saying aloud something he'd never dared admit to himself. 'To get the painting and sell it and spend all the money with you . . .'

'One and a half million dollars, maybe a little more, as you well know.' Toussaints Morton also moved closer to Biralbo, lowering his voice. 'But there's a slight problem, my friend. That money is ours. We want it. Understand? Now.'

'I don't know what money or what picture you're talking about.' Biralbo leant back on the sofa so that Morton was no longer breathing in his face. He was calm, a little drowsy from the gin, almost completely detached from himself and from his surroundings, a little impatient. 'What I do know is that Lucrecia didn't have a penny. Nothing. I gave her all my money so she could leave San Sebastian.'

'So that she could come here, to Lisbon, don't you mean? Two former lovers meet again and go on a long journey together . . .'

'I didn't ask her where she was going.'

'You didn't need to.' Toussaints Morton stopped smiling. Now he looked incapable of it. 'I know you left together. I even know that it was you driving the car. Would you like me to tell you the exact date? Daphne must have it written in her diary.'

'Lucrecia was running away from you.' For a while now Biralbo had been longing for a cigarette. Slowly he brought out a packet and his lighter, and lit one, holding Malcolm's steady gaze. 'She was afraid you'd kill her just like you killed that man, the Portuguese.'

Toussaints Morton listened, as if he were waiting for a punch-line, ready to laugh, smiling again and hunching his shoulders a little. At last he burst out laughing and slapped his thighs with his huge palms.

'Do you really expect us to believe that?' He stared gravely at Biralbo and Malcolm as though they both deserved his pity. 'Are you telling me that Lucrecia said nothing about the map she stole from us? That you know nothing about Burma?'

'He's lying,' said Malcolm. 'Leave him to me. I'll make him tell us the truth.'

'Calm down, Malcolm.' Toussaints Morton waved him away from Biralbo with a loud jangling of gold bracelets. 'I'm beginning to suspect that our friend Biralbo is not as dumb as you . . . And would you mind telling me something?' Now he sounded like a kind and patient policeman, almost merciful. 'Lucrecia was scared of us. Very well. I'm sorry about that but I understand. She was afraid and she fled because she saw us kill a man. The human race suffered no great loss that night, but you will point out, quite rightly, that this isn't the time to go into those questions. I simply want to ask you one thing: why didn't the fair Lucrecia – so horri-fied by a crime she shouldn't have witnessed – go straight to the police? She could easily have done so. She'd escaped from us, she knew the exact location of the corpse. But she didn't. Can't you guess why?'

Biralbo said nothing. He was thirsty and his eyes stung from the smoke in the room. Daphne was looking at him with interest, as one might peer at the passenger in the next seat. He had to remain firm, not even blink, like he knew everything but was pretending ignorance. He remembered one of Lucrecia's letters, the last one: an envelope he found empty, received several months after he had left San Sebastian for good. 'Burma, Burma,' he repeated to himself, pronouncing a spell he didn't understand, a mysterious, sacred word.

'Burma,' said Toussaints Morton. 'It's a shame there's no respect any more. Somebody hired the premises, appropriated the name and turned it into a brothel. When we saw the sign in the street I said to Daphne, "What would the late Dom Bernardo Ulhman Ramires think if he saw this?" But I can tell that you don't even know who Dom Bernardo was. Young people today know nothing and think it doesn't matter. Dom Bernardo himself once told me, in Zurich — I can picture him as clearly as I see you — "Morton," he said, "for men of my generation and my class, the end of the world has arrived. Our only solace is collecting beautiful paintings and books, and visiting foreign spas." You should have heard the majesty with which he said, for instance, "Oswald Spengler", or "Asia", or "Civilization". He owned entire jungles in Angola and coffee plantations bigger than Portugal. And what a palace, my friend, on an island in the middle of a lake — I never saw it, unfortunately, but I'm told it was made entirely of marble, like the Taj Mahal. Dom Bernardo Ulhman Ramires was not a landowner, he was the head of a magnificent kingdom built in the jungle. I expect they've turned it all into a commune of malaria-ridden beggars by now. Dom Bernardo loved the Orient, loved great art, and he wanted his collection to rival the best in Europe. "Morton," he'd say to me, "when I see a picture I like, how much I have to pay to get it isn't important." He loved French painting and old maps more than anything. He was capable of going across the world to examine a painting. And I found them for him. Not just me – he had a dozen agents scouring Europe for paintings and maps. Name a great master, any one: Dom Bernardo Ulhman Ramires had a painting or drawing by him. He also loved opium. Why deny it? It takes away none of his nobility. During the war he worked for the British in south-east Asia and returned with a taste for opium and a collection of pipes that will never be rivalled. He liked to recite a Portuguese poem. One of the lines went like this: "*Um Oriente ao oriente do Oriente . . .*" Am I boring you? I'm sorry, I'm a sentimentalist. I despise a civilization that has no place for a man such as Dom Bernardo Ulhman Ramires. I know, I know, you disapprove of imperialists. In that too, you resemble Malcolm. You see the colour of my skin and think, "Toussaints Morton must hate colonial empires." But you're mistaken, my friend. Do you know where I would be if it weren't for imperialism, as Malcolm puts it? Not here, for sure, which would be a great relief to you. I'd be up a palm tree in Africa, like a monkey. I'd play a tom-tom, and make masks out of bark . . . I'd know nothing of Rossini or Cézanne. And please don't mention the Noble Savage, I beg you!'

'Let him tell us about the Cézanne,' said Malcolm. 'And what he and Lucrecia did with it.'

'My dear Malcolm,' Toussaints Morton smiled with papal equanimity. 'One day your impatience will be your undoing. I have an idea: let's recruit our friend Biralbo into our happy little company. We can offer him a deal. Let's accept that his business relationship with the fair Lucrecia may not have been as satisfactory as their personal one . . . Here's the proposal, my friend, my best and last offer: you help us retrieve what is rightfully ours and you get a cut when we divide the profits. Do you recall, Daphne? We made the same offer to the Portuguese . . .'

'We're not making a deal with him,' said Malcolm. 'Not while I'm here. He thinks he can trick us, Toussaints, he was smiling while you were talking. Tell us where the picture is, where the money is, Biralbo. Tell us or I'll kill you. Right now.'

He was gripping the gun so tightly that his knuckles were white and his hand shook. Daphne stood up and moved slowly away from Biralbo, sliding her back along the wall. 'Malcolm,' said Toussaints Morton quietly. 'Malcolm.' But Malcolm wasn't listening, or looking at him. He was staring into Biralbo's calm eyes, demanding fear and submission, silently affirming as rigidly as he held the gun the continuation of the old grudge, the useless, almost shared anger at having lost the right to his memories and the dignity of failure.

'Stand up,' he said, and when Biralbo was on his feet put the gun to his chest. Close up it looked huge and obscene, like a chunk of iron. 'Talk or I'll kill you right now.'

Biralbo told me later that he'd spoken, not knowing what he was saying, and that at that moment terror had made him invulnerable. He said, 'Go on, Malcolm, fire. You'd be doing me a favour.'

'Where have I heard that before?' said Toussaints Morton. His voice seemed to come from another room. Biralbo saw nothing but Malcolm's eyes.

'In *Casablanca*,' said Daphne, precisely, indifferently. 'Humphrey Bogart says it to Ingrid Bergman.'

Hearing this Malcolm's face was transformed. He looked at Daphne, forgetting about the gun, genuine rage and cruelty contracting his mouth, and his eyes had narrowed when he turned them back on Biralbo.

'Movies,' he said, almost incomprehensibly. 'That was the only

thing that mattered to you, wasn't it? You despised anyone who
didn't know about films, you talked about them and your books
and your songs but I knew you were talking about yourselves. You
didn't care about anyone or anything, reality was too ordinary for
you. Isn't that right?'

Biralbo saw Malcolm's large body moving closer, as if about to
collapse on top of him, his eyes so near they seemed distorted.
Biralbo stepped back, bumping into the sofa. Malcolm was still
bearing down on him like a landslide. Biralbo kicked him in the
stomach, moving out of the way to avoid his falling body and, suddenly, Malcolm's hand, still holding the gun, was in front of him.
He struck or bit it, and everything went dark. When he opened his
eyes he was holding the gun. Malcolm was still hunched over, on
his knees, his face against the sofa, and Daphne and Toussaints
Morton were staring, edging away. 'Calm down, my friend,'
Morton said quietly, 'calm down.' But he wasn't smiling, he was
staring nervously at the gun now pointed at him. Biralbo took a few
steps back and felt for the lock on the door. Malcolm turned
towards him, slowly getting to his feet. Biralbo finally managed to
get the door open. He backed out, remembering that was how it
was done by heroes in films, slammed the door shut and ran
towards the metal stairs. Only as he crossed the pink gloom of the
bar, where blonde women sat drinking, did he realize that he was
still holding the gun and that several pairs of eyes were staring at
him in surprise and fear.

He came out on to the street and as the damp night air struck his face he realized why he wasn't afraid: if he'd lost Lucrecia then nothing mattered. He put the heavy gun in his coat pocket and stopped, overcome by a strange inertia, like the paralysis in dreams. Above him the sign of the Burma Club flashed on and off, illuminating a tall building with empty balconies. He set off at a brisk walk, hands in his pockets, as though late for an appointment. He couldn't run because the street was as crowded as the quayside of an Asiatic port, with faces coloured blue and green by the neon lights, sphinx-like women standing alone, groups of black men appearing to move to a beat they alone could hear, gangs of men with coppery skin and oriental features who seemed to congregate there out of a hazy nostalgia for the cities whose names hung along the street: Shanghai, Hong Kong, Goa, Jakarta.

He felt the lethal calm of someone who knows he's drowning, and turned to look at the sign of the Burma, still so close he seemed not to have moved. The seconds felt like hours and he scanned the countless faces, searching for Malcolm, Toussaints Morton, Daphne, even Lucrecia, knowing he should run but lacking the will, like someone trying to wake up but who keeps dropping off. He told me that the gun was so heavy and there were so many faces and bodies, that making his way through the crowd was like advancing through thick jungle undergrowth. In that instant Biralbo turned and saw Malcolm's cold, blue eyes. Malcolm had seen him too, but was moving forwards just as slowly, as if swimming against a powerful current, taller than those around him, staring at Biralbo like the shore he was struggling towards. Unable to stop looking at each other, they both slowed, running into people, sometimes swallowed by the crowd which broke their gaze. But they made contact again, and the street seemed to stretch on for ever, eventually becoming darker, with fewer faces and club signs. Suddenly Biralbo saw Malcolm still and alone in an empty roadway, standing in front of his own shadow, legs apart, and then he did start running. The narrow streets opened up before him like a highway in the headlights of a car. Behind him he could hear Malcolm's footsteps, even the sound of his breathing, at once very distant and very close, like a threat or a plea in the silence of the resplendent, empty squares, the vast colonnades and streets lined with shops, where their steps sounded in unison. As exhaustion choked him, his sense of space and time disintegrated. He was in Lisbon and San Sebastian, he was running away from Malcolm just as on another identical night he fled from Toussaints Morton, through a dual city that conjured up its network of streets to turn itself into a maze and an endless chase.

And then suddenly the streets were identical and geometric, partially abandoned stretches leading to brightly lit squares from which floated the weak but essential sound of an inhabited city. He ran towards the lights as though towards an ever-receding mirage. Behind him the slow rumble of a tram drowned out Malcolm's footsteps and he saw it pass, tall, yellow, looking as empty as a ship adrift at sea, and stop a little further on. Maybe he could catch it. Someone got out, the tram paused and Biralbo was almost level when it set off again slowly, swaying. He stood motionless watching the tram pull away from the station, mouth and eyes wide open, wiping the sweat from his face and the saliva from his lips, forgetting about Malcolm and the need to run. With an immense effort, he turned and saw that Malcolm too had stopped, standing only a few yards away on the opposite kerb, as if on the ledge of a tall building, about to plunge off, panting and coughing and pushing his red hair out of his eyes. Biralbo felt the butt of the gun. In a sudden hallucination, he saw himself pointing it at Malcolm, and he almost heard the shot and the dull thud of the body falling on to the tram rails; it would be as easy as closing his eyes, never moving again, dying. But Malcolm was coming towards him, as though his feet were sinking in sand with each step. He tried running again, but didn't have the strength. To his left he saw a dark side street, a flight of steps and a slender tower, taller than the surrounding houses, alone, rising absurdly above them, with gothic windows and iron ribs. He went towards the light in a doorway where a ticket collector with a pouch full of coins on his belt handed him a ticket. 'Fifteen escudos,' he said, and pushed Biralbo inside. Slowly he pulled shut a rusty iron gate and turned a copper handle, and the whole structure, which Biralbo hadn't yet looked at, shuddered and creaked like a steam ship, and began to rise.

There was a face at the gate, two hands gripping and shaking it – Malcolm, sinking, disappearing from view before Biralbo had time to fully realize that he was in a lift and no longer needed to run.

The ticket collector, a woman with a scarf on her head and a man with white sideburns, wearing a sombre raincoat, all stared at him with intense disapproval. The woman had a very wide face and was chewing something. Slowly and methodically she examined Biralbo's muddy shoes, untucked shirt, flushed and sweaty face. He kept his hand hidden in his coat pocket. Beyond the gothic windows the city opened out and grew smaller as the lift rose. White squares like lakes of light, illuminated signs on rooftops, the blackness of the estuary, buildings on a hill topped by a harshly floodlit castle.

The lift stopped and he asked where they were. 'The upper town,' the ticket collector told him. Flights of steps and walls of abandoned houses dropped away steeply. Malcolm might still be walking along those streets down below. Biralbo emerged into a passageway where a sea wind blew, cold as on a ship's deck. Beside the tower of a ruined church was a taxi that looked as strange and still as an insect surprised by the light. He asked the driver to take him to the station and out of the rear window watched for the headlights of another car, checking the faces on dark street corners. Exhausted, he fell back against the hard plastic seat and wished the taxi journey would never end. With his eyes half closed, he sank into the city as if it were an underwater landscape, recognizing places, statues, signs on old shops or department stores, the entrance of his hotel, which he felt he had left a long time ago.

All Lisbon, he told me – even the stations – is a maze of steps that never quite reach the highest places: there was always a cupola or a tower or a row of inaccessible yellow houses above you. He went up escalators and along passageways past filthy urinals to get to the platform where, every morning, he caught the train to go and see Billy Swann.

Several times he thought he was still being followed. Everywhere he looked was a concealed enemy. He got off at the last stop and when there was nobody left at the platform, drank a glass of brandy at the bar. He avoided looking at the ticket inspectors and waiters. He imagined conspiracy in their eyes and in the incomprehensible talk all around him, and they stared at him: perhaps recognizing him, or maybe they guessed he was a fugitive and a foreigner. When he saw himself in the mirror above a washbasin his face frightened him. His hair was wild, his face very pale and his tie hung like a noose around his neck, but what scared him most was the strange look in his eyes. They no longer saw things as they had a few hours earlier. There seemed to be pity in them and a premonition of his own doom. 'It's me,' he said aloud, watching the lips moving in the mirror. 'Santiago Biralbo.'

The dark places, the conical towers of the castle surrounded by rooftops and columns of smoke, the road through the forest, preserved a mysterious stillness and quiet identity confirmed by the secrecy of the night. At the entrance to the hospital a man was loading bags and suitcases into a car – a big, gleaming taxi completely unlike those in Lisbon. 'Oscar,' said Biralbo; the man turned, not having recognized Biralbo in the dark. He placed the double bass carefully on the back seat and smiled, wiping his forehead with a handkerchief that, like his teeth, was a luminous white in the darkness.

'We're leaving,' he said. 'Tonight. Billy's decided he's feeling better. I was going to call you at your hotel. You know what he's like, he wants us to start rehearsing tomorrow.'

'Where is he?'

'Inside. Saying goodbye to the nun. I'm afraid he's determined to give her his last bottle of whisky.'

'Is it true that he's stopped drinking?'

'Everything except orange juice. He says he's dead. "The dead don't drink, Oscar." That's what he says to me. He smokes a lot and drinks orange juice.'

Oscar turned away abruptly and went back inside. When he re-emerged, Biralbo was leaning against the taxi's open door, staring at him.

'Oscar, I need to ask you something.'

'Go ahead. You sound like a police interrogator.'

'Who's paid the hospital bill?'

'Ask him.' Without looking at Biralbo, Oscar moved away, as if he felt too close, and wiped the sweat from his hands with the handkerchief. 'There he is.'

'Oscar.' Biralbo stood in front of him, forcing him to stop. 'He told you to lie to me, didn't he? He wouldn't let you tell me that Lucrecia's been here . . .'

'What's going on?' Tall and frail, wrapped up in a coat with his hat pulled right down to his glasses, Billy Swann came towards them out of the light, a cigarette between his lips and trumpet case in his hand. 'Oscar, tell the driver we're ready to leave.'

'Right, Billy.' Oscar obeyed with the relief of someone who's managed to avoid punishment. He treated Billy Swann with a reverence not always distinguishable from fear.

'Billy,' said Biralbo, noticing his voice shook, like he'd had a lot to drink or a sleepless night. 'Tell me where she is.'

'You don't look too good, son.' Billy Swann was very close, but Biralbo couldn't see his eyes, only the gleam of his glasses. 'You look closer to death than I do. Aren't you pleased to see me? Old Billy Swann is back in the land of the living.'

'I need to know about Lucrecia, Billy. Tell me where I can find her. She's in danger.'

Billy Swann tried to push past him and get into the taxi, but Biralbo didn't move. In the darkness he couldn't see the expression on Billy Swann's face, a pale, inscrutable emptiness beneath the brim of his hat. But Billy Swann could see Biralbo's face in the lights from the entrance hall. He put the trumpet case down and threw his cigarette away after one last drag, the thin, hard lines of his lips visible as the ember glowed. Very slowly he took off his gloves, flexing his fingers as though they were numb.

'If you could only see your face now, son. You're the one in danger.'

'I haven't got all night, Billy. I have to find her before they do. They're going to kill her. They nearly killed me.'

He heard a door close and then voices and footsteps on the gravel path. Oscar and the taxi driver were heading towards them.

'Come with us,' said Billy Swann. 'We can take you back to your hotel.'

'You know I'm not going to, Billy.' The taxi driver started the engine, but Biralbo didn't move from the car door. He was cold, slightly feverish, feeling urgency and dizziness. 'Tell me where I can find Lucrecia.'

'When you're ready, Billy.' Oscar leant his large, curly head out of the window and looked suspiciously at Biralbo.

'That woman's no good for you, boy,' said Billy Swann, moving him aside firmly. He opened the taxi door and placed the trumpet case on the front seat, crisply telling the driver he needn't be in such a hurry. He spoke in English, but the man seemed to understand and switched off the engine. 'Maybe it's not her fault. Maybe it's something in you that has nothing to do with her, leading you to destruction. Like whisky or heroin. You know I know what I'm talking about. I can see it in your eyes. They look like mine after a week holed up with a crate of booze. Get in the taxi. Go back to your hotel. We'll play on the twelfth and then leave Lisbon. Once you're on the plane it'll be as if you were never here.'

'You don't understand, Billy. It's not for me, it's for her. They're going to kill her if they find her.'

Billy Swann got into the taxi, without taking his hat off, and placed the black trumpet case on his knees. He didn't shut the door. As if playing for time he lit a cigarette and took a long drag.

'You think it's you who's been looking for her, that you saw her on the train by chance the other day. But she's been trying to find you. I didn't want you to know. I forbade her to see you. She did as I told her because she's scared of me, like Oscar. Do you remember that concert hall in Stockholm where we played before going to America? She was there, in the audience. She'd travelled from Lisbon to see us. To see you, I mean. And after that, in Hamburg, she left my dressing room five minutes before you arrived. She was the one who brought me here and paid the medical bill in advance. She's got a lot of money now. She lives alone. I expect she's waiting for you. She told me how to get to her house. A train leaves the station here every twenty minutes for the coast. Get off when you see a lighthouse, the stop before last. You have to walk about half a mile, with the lighthouse behind you, keeping the sea on your left. She said the house has a tower and a walled garden. There's a name on the gate. Don't ask me what it is — it's in Portuguese and

I can never remember a word of that language. House of the Wolves or something.'

'I remember it,' said Oscar, from the darkness. 'Quinta dos Lobos.'

Billy Swann closed the taxi door and stared at Biralbo as he wound up the window. For a moment, as the driver swung the car round to head down the tree-lined driveway, one of the lights along the drive shone straight into Billy Swann's face. It was thin and rigid, unfamiliar, as if the man who'd spoken to him from the shadows had been an impostor.

I remember him talking for several hours in his hotel room that last night, high on tobacco and words. He only stopped to light a cigarette, or take quick sips from a glass containing little more than melting ice, possessed beyond hope at three or four in the morning by the places and names he'd at first invoked so dispassionately. He was resolved to go on until the night was over — not just this night in Madrid, but also another, the one he'd conjured with his words, that had taken hold of us like an enemy in disguise. He wasn't telling the story: it had trapped him surreptitiously, just as music sometimes did, and gave him no choice but to continue talking. But neither his slow, calm voice nor his eyes betrayed any of this. He didn't look at me as he talked, staring at his cigarette, or the ice in his glass, or the closed curtains, which I parted from time to time to see, without relief, that no one was watching from across the street. He seemed to be talking about someone else's life, sounding detached, thorough, as though making an official statement. Perhaps he wanted to continue till the end because he knew we would never see each other again.

'Once I knew where Lucrecia was,' he said, 'and Billy Swann's taxi had left and I was alone on the road through the forest, everything was as it had always been – like in San Sebastian when I'd arranged to meet her, the hours or the minutes until I saw her again seemed to stretch on interminably and the bar or hotel where we were meeting was on the other side of the world. I felt the same fear, that she'd left and that I wouldn't be able to find her. At first, in San Sebastian, on my way to her, I'd look in all the taxis that passed in front of mine, afraid of seeing Lucrecia in one of them . . .'

He realized that it wasn't true one forgets. The only truth, which he'd driven from his mind since leaving San Sebastian, had taken refuge in his dreams, where his will and his bitterness couldn't touch it; in his dreams, where he saw Lucrecia, and her face as it used to be, her invincible tenderness, as he had known her before they had lost their courage and their right to desire and innocence. In Stockholm, New York, Paris, after weeks without thinking of her, waking in unfamiliar hotels, aroused or gratified by the fleeting presence of other women, he remembered and then lost again dreams in which a gentle sadness cast its light over the perfect happiness of his best days with her and the vivid colours the world had seemed to have. As in those dreams, he searched for her now and sensed her presence in the night-time landscape of trees and hills he travelled through towards the sea. He peered anxiously at any light he saw, afraid of missing the lighthouse. It was past midnight and the carriage was empty. The ticket inspector had said the penultimate station was still ten minutes away. Through the window at the end he could see the metal bars of the next carriage, which seemed empty too. He looked at his watch but couldn't work out how many minutes had passed since he'd spoken to the ticket inspector. He was about to put on his coat when, through the window at the end of the carriage, he saw Malcolm's face pressed to the glass, watching him.

He got up. His muscles felt stiff and his knees ached. The train was going so fast it was almost impossible to stay standing; Malcolm stood with his feet far apart for balance, while in front of him the carriage door swung and banged, pushed by a sudden cold gust that reached Biralbo, bringing with it the monotonous sound of the wheels on the rails, and wood and metal joints creaking as though uncoupling when the train went round a curve. He ran down the corridor, holding on to the seats to steady himself, and tried to open the door at the far end of the carriage but it was impossible and Malcolm was so close he could see his blue eyes shining brightly. Absurdly, he kept tugging the door towards him, unable to open it, until a sudden jolt threw him forward and he found himself suspended, dizzy with terror, over a platform that shifted and seemed to open up beneath his feet, in the gap between the two carriages. Below, in blackness, the rails sparked. A piercing wind took his breath away, pushing him against a handrail which only just reached his waist and which he managed to grab just as he felt that, as if convulsing to vomit, he would be flung on to the tracks.

He turned. Malcolm was a step behind, on the other side of the door. In a single, lightning-fast movement he had to let go of the handrail and reach the door of the next carriage, without looking down at the metal plates shifting above the curving pebble path that disappeared into the darkness. He closed his eyes and jumped, and the door opened and closed behind him with a hermetic click. He ran through the deserted carriage towards another door and another oval window: it seemed the succession of rows of empty seats and yellow lights and black abysses sliced by wind would never end, that the train was travelling only for him to go in search of Lucrecia pursued by Malcolm, whom he could no longer see; perhaps he hadn't yet managed to jump from the other wagon. Then he heard banging and saw Malcolm's face at the oval window, kicking the door which he finally managed to open, coming towards Biralbo with his hair blown about in the wind. Again Biralbo went into the dark, holding on to the freezing handrail with both hands, but there was no door further on, just a grey metal partition, he'd reached the engine coupling, and Malcolm was slowly getting closer, leaning forwards as if into the wind.

He remembered the gun: when he went for it, he realized he'd left it in his coat. If the train slowed maybe he could jump. But the train raced as if headlong down a hill and Malcolm was already opening the only door that stood between them. Biralbo leant back against the corrugated metal and watched Malcolm approaching like he would never reach him, as though the speed of the train was holding them apart. There was no gun in Malcolm's open hands. He was moving his lips, perhaps shouting, but the wind and the noise of the train drowned out his words and their futile rage. His feet far apart and his hands open, he flung himself or was impelled towards Biralbo. They seemed to be embracing rather than fighting, or leaning against each other to stop themselves falling. They slipped and fell to their knees, then rose, entangled, only to fall again, propelled together towards the void. Biralbo heard breathing, unsure if it was his own or

Malcolm's, and swearing in English that could have come from either of them. He felt hands, nails, blows, the weight of a body, the distant feeling of his head slammed against metal. He stood up seeing lights, blinded by a warm liquid running down his forehead. He wiped his eyes and saw Malcolm getting slowly to his feet, as though lifting himself out of mud, his coat and trousers torn. Taller and less distinct than ever, Malcolm loomed over Biralbo, swaying, stretching his huge hands towards his neck, and when Biralbo moved out of the way, for a moment he seemed to lean over the handrail, looking out at the steep embankment and dark night. Biralbo saw him wave his arms like the wings of a bird, saw a look of astonishment and entreaty on Malcolm's face when the train jerked as if it might overturn and Biralbo fell to the metal-plate floor: he heard a long, piercing scream that echoed the screeching of the brakes, and he closed his eyes, as if the voluntary darkness could save him from hearing it any more.

He stayed pressed against the floor, trembling so much he wouldn't have known how to stand. He saw isolated houses among the trees, cars waiting at level crossings. The train had slowed down slightly. Still trembling, Biralbo got to his knees, wiping the dark trickle from his face and feeling for a handhold to help himself up. When the train had almost come to a halt he saw, high up beyond the trees, a light that appeared and disappeared with the slow, precise rhythm of a pendulum. As if emerging from a dream or amnesia he remembered with surprise where he was and why he was there.

He jumped on to the tracks to avoid being seen and headed away from the station lights, between abandoned carriages, tripping on rails overgrown with weeds. He climbed over a rotten fence, and slipped and fell as he ascended an embankment. He could no longer see the station or the lighthouse. The ground was uneven, and soaking wet. Frozen to the bone, he advanced through scattered trees, giving a wide berth to houses with barking dogs and making his way round garden walls that blocked his path. Skirting one which seemed never to end, he realized he was lost. He was in a tidy, ordinary street, with locked wrought-iron gates, streetlights on the corners and plastic litter bins. With torn clothes and his face covered in blood, he was sure that anyone who saw him would call the police. But he hadn't the energy or the will to think of anything to do but walk straight down the street, hoping he would hear or smell the sea, or glimpse the lighthouse through the eucalyptus trees.

The street was long and straight, obviously running parallel to the coast road. At times Biralbo heard cars close by and felt a faint breath of sea air on his face. The identical walls of the houses gave way to muddy, open ground where the scaffolding of a building under construction stood out against the clear night sky. To one side was the main road, and then the lighthouse and the cliffs. He moved away from the road to avoid the car headlights and walked almost along the edge of the cliff. Far below, spray rose, phosphorescent against the rocks. He looked away, afraid of the depths that seemed to beckon to him. The lighthouse shone like a large, yellow summer moon, a revolving polyhedron of light that multiplied his shadow and disconcerted him when it died. Head down, hands in his pockets, he walked on obstinately, like a tramp wandering the streets, his upturned collar the only protection against the cold sea wind. He had left the lighthouse far behind by the time he saw, above the pines, the house Billy Swann described. A long wall invisible from the road, a half-open gate, and the name: Quinta dos Lobos.

He entered, afraid of barking dogs. The gate opened silently when he pushed it and crossing the indistinct garden all he could hear were his footsteps on the gravel. He saw a tower, a small porch with columns, a light in a window. He stopped at the door, with the same feeling of emptiness and helplessness he had on the train platform and along the cliff. He rang the bell but nothing happened. He rang again. This time he heard it, deep inside the house. Then silence, the wind in the trees. He was certain he heard footsteps and that someone was standing behind the door. 'Lucrecia,' he said as if trying to wake her gently. 'Lucrecia.'

I can't imagine the face that Biralbo saw then, or the moment of recognition or tenderness between them. I never saw them together and I could never picture it. What unites them, and what may unite them still, was a bond based on secrecy. They never had witnesses, not even when they no longer needed to hide. If someone I didn't know had been with them or come across them in one of those hidden bars or hotels where they used to meet in San Sebastian, I'm sure he wouldn't have observed anything at all of what really passed between them: the mesh of words and gestures, of greed and restraint. They never believed they deserved each other, and they never wanted or had anything except what was within themselves, a shared, invisible kingdom, rarely visited but impossible to renounce, because its borders surrounded them as inevitably as skin or smell forms the outline of a body. When they looked at each other they belonged to each other, the same way you know yourself when you look in a mirror.

They stood for a moment, on the threshold, not embracing or saying a word, as if facing strangers. More beautiful, almost unrecognizable with very short hair and in a silk blouse, Lucrecia opened the door wide to look at him in the full light, and told him to come in. Perhaps at first there was a distance between them that common memories couldn't diminish, a cowardly, anxious politeness that had so often made them strangers when a single word or caress would have brought them together.

'What happened to you?' asked Lucrecia. 'How did you hurt your face?'

'You have to leave here.' Biralbo touched his forehead and brushed her hand as she was pushing away his hair to look at the wound. 'They're looking for you. They'll find you if you don't leave.'

'Your lip's cut.' Lucrecia was touching his face but he couldn't feel it. She was so close he could smell her hair, and see the colour of her eyes, but he saw it all as if from a great distance, or fainting – if he moved, if he took one step, he would fall over. 'You're shaking. Here, lean on me.'

'Give me a drink. And a cigarette. I'm dying for a smoke. I left my cigarettes in my coat. With the gun. I'm such a fool.'

'What gun? No, don't talk. Lean on me.'

'Malcolm's. He was going to shoot me but I took it. In the most ridiculous way.'

He only sensed his surroundings intermittently, clarity alternating rapidly with drowsiness. If he closed his eyes he was back on the train, and felt he would collapse from dizziness. As he walked, leaning on Lucrecia, he caught sight of himself in a mirror – his bloodied face and red-rimmed eyes scared him. She helped him lie back on a sofa, in an empty room where a fire was burning. When he opened his eyes Lucrecia was gone. She returned with a bottle and two glasses. She knelt by his side, wiped his face with a damp towel and put a cigarette between his lips.

'Did Malcolm do this to you?'

'I fell against something metal. Or maybe he pushed me, I don't know. It was very dark. I kept standing up and falling over again, and he was trying to hit me. Poor Malcolm. He really had it in for me. And he was crazy about you.'

'Where is he now?'

'In the next world, I suppose. On the tracks, if there's anything left of him. I can still hear him scream.'

'Did you kill him?'

'I don't know. I may have, I pushed him, but I'm not sure. Maybe they've already found the body. You have to get out of here.'

'Did anyone follow you?'

'Toussaints Morton is going to find you if you don't leave. When he reads the paper tomorrow he'll know where to look. It might take him a week or a month, but he'll find you. Get out of here, Lucrecia.'

'How can I leave now that you're here?'

'Anybody could get in. You hadn't even locked the gate.'

'I left it open for you.'

Biralbo downed his glass of bourbon in one gulp and sat up, leaning on Lucrecia's shoulders. He realized she'd thought he was going to put his arms round her and that was why she smiled when she leant towards him. The bourbon made his lip sting, and its slow, pleasant warmth revived him. It was a long time since he'd seen that look on Lucrecia's face: alert to every detail of his presence, almost overcome by the intensity of her own gaze, by the fear that any slight gesture might be a signal that he was leaving. But she wasn't a memory. He shuddered as he realized that for the first time he was seeing in Lucrecia's eyes an expression only Malcolm had witnessed. What his memory had failed to retain was now restored to him through the jealousy of a dead man.

He washed his face with cold water in a large bathroom, which, in the gleam of the porcelain and the faucets, had the air of an old-fashioned operating theatre. His bottom lip was swollen and there was a gash on his forehead. He combed his hair carefully and adjusted his tie as if he was getting ready for a date with Lucrecia. On his way back he looked around for the first time: in all the rooms the objects seemed to be arranged so as to emphasize the emptiness, the feeling of space and solitude. Guided by faint music, he found his way back to Lucrecia without getting lost in the corridors.

'Who's that playing?' he asked. The music offered solace as warm and sweet as a summer night, as the memory of a happy dream.

'You,' said Lucrecia. 'You and Billy Swann. "Lisbon". Don't you recognize your own playing? I've always wondered how you wrote that song without ever having been to Lisbon.'

'That's exactly why I could do it. I couldn't now.'

He sat on the corner of the sofa, in the middle of the empty room, facing the fire. There was a single shelf of books and records, a low table with a lamp and typewriter, and a stereo system at the far end with red and green lights behind black glass panels. No matter how much they have, he thought, truly solitary people create emptiness wherever they live and in whatever paths they travel. Lucrecia sat at the other end of the sofa, smoking, listening to the music, eyes half closed, opening them sometimes to look tenderly at Biralbo.

'I have a story to tell you,' she said.

'I don't want to hear it. I've heard too many tonight.'

'You need to know. This time it's the whole truth.'

'I can guess.'

'They told you about the picture, didn't they? The map I took.'

'You don't understand, Lucrecia. I didn't come to hear this. I don't want to know why they're after you or why you sent me that map of Lisbon. I came to tell you that you've got to get away. When I finish this drink I'm leaving.'

'I don't want you to go.'

'I've got a rehearsal with Billy Swann tomorrow. We're playing on the twelfth.'

Lucrecia moved closer. The habits of courage and solitude she had acquired had made her eyes larger. Her short hair gave her features a definition and truth that they may have had before only in adolescence. She was about to say something, but pressed her lips together with a look of futility and resignation, and stood up. Biralbo watched her walk over to the shelf. She returned with a book and opened it in front of him. It was a large volume of glossy reproductions of paintings. Lucrecia pointed at one of them, resting the book against the typewriter. Biralbo told me that looking at that painting was like hearing music which was almost silence, like being very slowly overcome by melancholy and joy. He understood suddenly that this was how he should play the piano, just like that man painted: with gratitude and restraint, wisdom and innocence, as if knowing everything and nothing, with the delicacy and fear of our first caress or necessary word. The colours dissolved in water or distance, a violet mountain, green patches that could have been trees, or shadows of trees on a summer's afternoon, a path disappearing into the hills, and a small solitary house with the outline of a window, almost hidden by an avenue of trees, as though someone had chosen to live there in hiding, to see nothing more than the peak of that mountain. 'Paul Cézanne,' he read at the bottom of the page, 'La Montagne Sainte Victoire, 1906; col. B. U. Ramires.'

'I had that picture,' said Lucrecia, closing the book suddenly. 'This reproduction gives you no idea of what it was really like. I had it and I sold it. I'll never get used to not having it any more.'

She stoked the fire, brought more cigarettes and filled their glasses slowly, calmly, ceremonially. The wind was beating on the windows, and the waves crashing against the cliffs sounded very close. Biralbo laid the book in his lap, staring at it while Lucrecia talked. Contemplating that landscape had suddenly changed everything: the night, his escape from Malcolm, his fear of dying, of not finding Lucrecia. The painting – like love sometimes, and music nearly always – made him understand the moral possibility of a strange, inexorable justice, an order, nearly always hidden, that shaped destiny and made the world habitable, but was not itself of this world. Sacred and mysterious but also ordinary and dissolved in the air, as when Billy Swann played his trumpet so softly that the sound lost itself in silence, like the ochre and pink and grey light at sunset in Lisbon: the feeling he was not decoding the meaning of the music or the patches of colour or the still, mysterious light, but that they understood and accepted him. But he'd learnt and then forgotten these things thirty years ago. He was rediscovering them now the way he knew them then, with more wisdom and less fervour, irredeemably linked to Lucrecia, to her serene voice and the way she smiled without parting her lips, to that perfume from the past that was like the fragrance of a lost homeland.

That was why he cared so little about her story. It was her voice that mattered, not her words; her presence, not the reason he was there with her. He felt everything that had happened since he arrived in Lisbon was like a gift. He raised his eyes from the book and looked at Lucrecia. Perhaps he didn't love her any more, didn't even desire her. But this coolness, freeing him from the past and from the ransom of grief, also enabled him to see her as he saw her in the days or hours before he fell in love with her, at the Lady Bird or the Vienna, or in some forgotten street in San Sebastian: so positive and expectant, as radiant as a city one is about to enter for the first time.

Once again he heard the words and names that had pursued him for so long. Even after that night their darkness remained intact, because it was more powerful than the truth or falsehood it contained: Lisbon, Burma, Ulhman, Morton, Cézanne, names which broke apart in Lucrecia's voice to regroup again in an unknown plot that partially modified and corrupted Biralbo's memories. Once again he heard the word 'Berlin' and all the connotations of distance and squalor and pain it had acquired during the years he'd spent writing letters to Lucrecia, thinking he would never see her again; a time when he surrendered to a life of mediocrity, decency, teaching at a convent school and going to bed early, while she watched a man being strangled with a nylon cord and escaped

through streets full of dirty snow in search of a postbox or someone to whom she could entrust her final letter to Biralbo,
containing that map of Lisbon, before Malcolm and Toussaints
Morton and Daphne could catch her . . .

'I lied to you,' said Lucrecia. 'You had a right to know but I
didn't tell you the truth. Or not the whole truth. If I had told you
it would have bound you to me, and I needed to be alone, to come
to Lisbon alone. I spent years tied to Malcolm, and then to you, to
your letters and my memories of you, I'd lost sight of my own life,
and I knew the only way I'd get it back was to be on my own.
That's why I lied and told you to leave when we were at that hotel;
it's what gave me the courage to steal the map and the gun from
Malcolm, and get away from him. I didn't care about him helping
Toussaints kill that drunk, it didn't increase my contempt or revul-
sion, it was no more sordid than his lying on top of me without
looking at me and heading for the bathroom afterwards with his
head down . . . He wanted us to have a child. From the moment the
Portuguese appeared on the scene, he talked about nothing else —
he was going to make lots of money, we could retire and have
children and not have to work for the rest of our lives. It make me
sick to think about it: a house with a garden, and Malcolm's child,
and Toussaints and Daphne coming to lunch every Sunday. I
remember the evening they first brought the Portuguese, held up
between them because he couldn't stand, as big as a tree, blond,
red, eyes bleary and shrunken like a pig's, drunk on beer, with
those tattoos on his arms. He was dropped on the sofa, breathing
hard and mumbling, slurring his words. Toussaints brought a case
of beer from the car and put it down next to the Portuguese, who
opened and drank the cans one by one, like an automaton, crush-
ing them in one hand as though they were paper and throwing

them on the floor. He kept repeating a word – "Burma" – which sometimes sounded like a place and others like the name of an army, or a conspiracy. Toussaints and Daphne didn't move from his side; they always had another beer ready for him, Daphne listening and taking notes, her folder in her lap. "Where's Burma?" Toussaints kept on asking the Portuguese, "In what part of Lisbon?", and once the Portuguese straightened, as if he'd sobered up, and said, "I won't talk. I won't break the promise I made to Dom Bernardo Ulhman Ramires before he died." He opened his eyes wide and looked round at all of us, tried to get up but just slumped back on the sofa and fell asleep like a big ox.'

'You have before you the last remaining soldier of a defeated army,' said Toussaints Morton solemnly, as if delivering a funeral oration. Lucrecia told of how, as he spoke about Dom Bernardo Ulhman Ramires and his defunct empire, Morton blew his nose noisily and tears welled up in his eyes. 'Real tears,' Lucrecia said. 'Huge glistening tears that ran down his face like drops of mercury.' While Daphne kept guard over the sleeping Portuguese, Toussaints Morton explained what Burma was and how they had the chance to get very rich by using a little ingenuity and cunning. 'Not brute force, Malcolm,' he warned. They just had to be patient. They must never leave the Portuguese on his own, and keep the fridge stocked with beer. 'All the beer in the world,' he said. He gestured towards the Portuguese. 'What would poor Dom Bernardo Ulhman Ramires think if he saw what's become of his best soldier?'

'A secret army,' said Lucrecia. 'The man had to get out of Angola after independence. He lost his coffee plantations and his palace in the middle of a lake and nearly all his paintings. He entered Portugal secretly and bought the biggest warehouse in Lisbon for his headquarters. That was what the Portuguese told Morton: that

Dom Bernardo sold the few paintings he had left to buy arms and sign up mercenaries, but after he died the Burma conspiracy gradually fell apart, and the warehouse was all that remained. That, not fear of the police, was why he left Lisbon. And he said something else: a small painting was still hanging in Dom Bernardo's office, beside an old calendar, but it couldn't be worth much because it hadn't been sold.'

'My friends,' said Toussaints Morton, checking that the Portuguese was still asleep in the next room. 'Do you think a collector with Dom Bernardo Ulhman Ramires's eye would have a worthless picture in his study? I, who knew him well, am sure he would not. That brute said it's a landscape, with a mountain and path. I trembled when I heard! I asked him discreetly if there was also a house among trees. I already knew he would say yes. I know that painting. Dom Bernardo showed it to me, fifteen years ago, in Zurich. And now it's hanging next to an old calendar, gathering dust in a warehouse in Lisbon, with no one to see it. Paul Cézanne painted it in nineteen hundred and six. Cézanne, Malcolm! Does the name mean anything to you? But it's irrelevant, you can't even imagine how much money we'd get for it if we find it . . .'

'But they didn't know where Burma was,' said Lucrecia, 'only that it was a coffee and spice warehouse, and that to get down into the basement you had to say the word "Burma". They kept the Portuguese drunk, not wanting to ask about it too directly in case he started to suspect something, but they must have lost patience, or maybe Malcolm said something that alerted him, because one day at the cabin they shut themselves in with him, I heard him shouting, and he came out putting something in his pocket — a crumpled sheet of paper. He staggered to the bathroom and stayed in there for ages, pissing so noisily it sounded like a horse . . .

Toussaints called out to him, very nervous, I think frightened the Portuguese had flushed the map down the toilet. "Come out," he said, "we'll split it with you fifty-fifty. You wouldn't know where to sell it on your own." I saw him put the nylon cord in his pocket. He looked at me and said, "Lucrecia, my dear, we're all hungry. Would you mind helping Daphne prepare lunch?"'

Biralbo stood up and poked the fire. The book still lay open against the typewriter. He thought the landscape had the same immutable gentleness as Lucrecia's eyes and voice. He imagined the painting hidden in the shadows, invisible to those who passed. It waited, motionless, faithful as a statue, unaffected by time or greed or crime. A single word was enough to obtain it, but it could only be said by the deserving.

'It was so easy,' said Lucrecia. 'As easy as crossing the road or getting on a bus. When I got to the warehouse there was almost no one around, just a few men loading old furniture and sacks of coffee on to a lorry. No one said anything when I went in; it was as if they couldn't see me. Inside there was an old-fashioned desk and a white-haired man writing in a big ledger, like he was entering the items the men were taking away, and I stood in front of him, my heart pounding, not knowing what to say. He took off his glasses to see me better and put them down on the book, and placed his pen in the inkwell, very careful not to mark what he'd written. He wore grey overalls. He asked what I wanted, very politely, like an elderly waiter, smiling at me. I said, "Burma." I thought he hadn't understood, because he just kept smiling. But then he shook his head and said quietly, "Burma doesn't exist any more. It stopped existing long before the police arrived." He put his glasses back on, took up his pen and started writing again. The men went on bringing things up

from the basement: sacks of coffee and boxes full of strange
things – boat lamps, coils of rope, copper objects, like navi-
gation equipment. I followed one of the men along a passage and
down a metal staircase. The picture was there, in a tiny office.
There were books and papers lying all over the floor. I closed the
door. I took the picture from its frame and put it in a plastic bag.
I felt as if I floated out of there. The white-haired man wasn't at
the desk. I saw his pen, the open ledger, his glasses. One of the
men loading the lorry said something and the others burst out
laughing but I ignored them. I spent two days locked in a hotel
room, touching the painting, almost caressing it. I wanted to
keep looking at it for ever.'

'Did you sell it in Lisbon?'

'No. Geneva. I knew where to go there. I sold it to a Texan who
didn't ask questions. I expect he's locked it up in a safe. Poor
Cézanne.'

'But I could have lost the letter,' said Biralbo after a long silence.
'Or thrown it away after reading it.'

'You know you would never have done that. I knew it too.'

'You took the map that night, at the hotel, didn't you? When I
went to hide Floro Bloom's car.'

'It was a motel. Do you remember what it was called?'

'It was in the middle of nowhere. I don't think it even had a
name.'

'But you didn't go out to hide the car.' Lucrecia seemed to be
enjoying testing Biralbo's memory. 'You said you had been out for
sandwiches.'

'We heard a car. Don't you remember? You were so scared you
went white. You thought Toussaints Morton had found us.'

'You were the one who was scared. And not of Toussaints

finding us. You were scared of me. As soon as we were alone in our room you suggested we go downstairs for a drink when there was a refrigerator full of drinks in the room. So then you thought of the sandwiches. You were terrified. I could see it in your eyes, in the way you moved.'

'It wasn't fear. It was simply desire.'

'Your hands were trembling when you lay down beside me. Your hands and lips. You'd turned off the light.'

'But it was you who turned it off. Of course I was trembling. Have you never felt almost unable to breathe you wanted someone so much?'

'Yes.'

'Don't tell me who.'

'You.'

'But that was at the beginning. The first night you came home with me. We were both trembling. We didn't touch each other, even in the dark. Because we didn't think we deserved what was happening.'

'We didn't deserve it.' Lucrecia emphasized her words by the way she lit a cigarette. She didn't do it herself: when it was between her lips, she offered the lighter to Biralbo in the palm of her hand so that he could take it and light it: that gesture alone denied nostalgia and celebrated the present. 'We were no better than we are now. We were too young. And immoral. What we were doing felt forbidden. We believed it was fate, so that excused us. Remember how we met in hotels, and how scared we were of Malcolm finding out, or your friends seeing us together.'

Biralbo shook his head. He said he didn't want to remember those sordid hours, the fear. Over the years he'd erased from his memory anything that might diminish or negate the two or three pivotal nights of his life. He didn't mind remembering, but he wanted to choose what he would always carry with him: that unforgettable night he came out of the Lady Bird with Lucrecia and Floro, hailed a taxi and got inside, burning with jealousy and cowardice, and Lucrecia opened the door and got in beside him and said, 'Malcolm's in Paris. I'm coming with you.' From the kerb, Floro Bloom, fat and smiling, huddled inside his big peacoat and waved goodbye.

'You were wearing a big coat too,' said Biralbo. 'It was black, very soft leather. The collar was so big it almost hid your face.'

'I left it in Berlin.' Now Lucrecia was as close to him as she had been in the taxi. 'It wasn't real leather. Malcolm gave it to me.'

'Poor Malcolm.' Biralbo remembered the flailing arms, searching vainly for something to hold on to. 'So he dealt in fake coats too?'

'He wanted to be a painter. He loved painting the way you love music. But painting didn't love him.'

'It was so cold that night. Your hands were frozen.'

'But it was not from the cold.' Now too Lucrecia felt for his hands, still looking at him: hers were as cold as his used to be when he got up on stage and first put them on the keyboard. 'I was afraid to touch you. I could feel your whole body and mine through your hands. Do you know when I thought about that again? When I left the warehouse with the Cézanne in a plastic bag. It seemed impossible and at the same time infinitely easy. Just as it was to get up one morning and steal the map and the gun from Malcolm and leave him for good.'

'That's why we weren't immoral,' said Biralbo. Now the relentless dizziness from the speeding train fused with the vertigo he had felt in the taxi that drove them, almost at dawn, through the hazy streets of San Sebastian. 'Because we only strove for the impossible.

We despised the mediocre, the kind of happiness others had. From the very first time we saw each other I could see in your eyes that you were dying to kiss me.'

'Not as much as now.'

'You're lying. Nothing will ever be better than what we had then.'

'It will be, because it's impossible.'

'I want you to lie to me,' said Biralbo. 'I don't want you ever to tell me the truth.' But as he spoke he was already brushing Lucrecia's lips.

W hen he opened his eyes it seemed he'd only been asleep for a few minutes. He remembered the abstract blue of the window, and the cold grey brightness that gradually tempered the light from the lamp, slowly sharpening outlines. But the colours remained indistinct, or dissolved altogether in the pale blue gloom, the whiteness of the sheets, the dull sheen of Lucrecia's warm skin. He'd felt – or maybe dreamt – that their bodies were growing, greedily occupying the entire space and, as they shook, disturbing the shadows that clung to them: on the verge of a shared, longed-for surrender they were revived by the quiet gratitude of accomplices. Maybe it wasn't that something was returned to them that night. Maybe, in that strange light that seemed to come out of nowhere, they found, as they looked at each other, something they hadn't been aware of, that they hadn't even desired until then:

the fervour with which they could discover each other in the
moments after the absolution of memory.

But he'd slept longer than a few minutes – the sun was shining
brightly through the translucent curtains. And it hadn't been a
dream, because Lucrecia was sleeping peacefully beside him, naked
under the sheet which wrapped her legs, dishevelled, her lips
parted, smiling perhaps, her profile sharp against the pillow, she
was as close to Biralbo as if she had fallen asleep when about to kiss
him.

He didn't move for fear of waking her. He looked around the
room, vaguely recognizing things, recovering from each one of
them the scattered details of what he couldn't remember: his
trousers lying on the floor, his shirt covered with small dark stains,
Lucrecia's high-heeled shoes, train tickets beside the ashtray on the
bedside table – clues to a night that suddenly seemed very distant,
neither terrifying nor propitious, simply unreal. Slowly, cautiously,
he began to sit up. Lucrecia stirred and said something in her sleep,
clinging to his waist. It must be very late; Billy Swann would be
trying to reach him at his hotel. Trying to get up without disturbing her, he turned over very slowly. As he slipped out of the bed
Lucrecia's hand lightly brushed his groin, then lay almost still on
the sheet feeling the space he'd vacated. She curled up and smiled
as if she was still holding him, and buried her face in the pillow,
hiding from the light and the need to wake.

Biralbo opened the shutters slightly. He realized that the feeling
of lightness which allowed him to move so quietly was not due to
his hours of sleep but the weight of the past being lifted. For the
first time in years he hadn't woken haunted by sorrow or a face he
had to recapture. He didn't call himself to account for the previous
night as he peered in the bathroom mirror. His lower lip was still

swollen and a narrow cut ran across his forehead, but even the baleful appearance of his unshaven face didn't seem too reprehensible. He could see the sea from the window, the waves gleaming like metal in the sun. Only one ordinary thing moved him: Lucrecia's red robe hanging on a hook. It smelt faintly of her skin and of bath salts.

In the past he would have searched bitterly, jealously, for signs of a male presence. Now, emerging from the shower, he was annoyed that he couldn't find anything to shave with. He examined with pleasure all the pots of creams, boxes of face powder, soaps, perfumes, and used with difficulty a sharp little razor that reminded him of a card-sharp's treacherous revolver. Hot water almost entirely washed away the bloodstains on his shirt. As he adjusted his tie he felt a sharp pain in his neck and suddenly remembered Malcolm. There was no remorse; he simply wanted to forget, to escape, like someone remembering he'd drunk too much the night before.

In the sitting room, the book on Cézanne lay open against the typewriter, beside an empty bottle and two glasses with a little water in the bottom. He looked again at the path, the violet mountain, the house among the trees, and they seemed immune to the slight taint affecting everything, even the hazy light over the sea. It was as if he'd taken too long to return to the home where he belonged. Everything was beginning to seem strange, unreal, and it gave him a feeling of freedom from lies, of liberty, of relief.

Searching for the kitchen to make coffee, he came instead to a room with three huge windows looking out over the cliffs. There was a table covered with books and handwritten pages, and another typewriter, with a blank sheet in the roller. Ashtrays, more books on the floor, empty cigarette packets, a plane ticket several months old: Lisbon–Stockholm–Lisbon. The pages, written in green ink, were covered in corrections. There was a photograph of a stranger on the wall; it was him, three or four years earlier, his eyes fixed on something that wasn't in that room or anywhere else, his hands at the keyboard of the piano at the Lady Bird. Half his face was in shadow; the other half showed fear, tenderness and a pure instinct for predicting the future. He wondered what Lucrecia thought and felt every night as she looked into those eyes that seemed to smile at whoever stood before them, and at the same time reject them, not even see them.

The house wasn't as big as it first seemed: it was drawn out by its emptiness and the wide horizon through the windows. He searched unsuccessfully for clues to Lucrecia's life. The silence, the white walls, the books, were his only answer. At the end of a passage he found the kitchen. It was clean and old-fashioned and seemed not to have been used in years. Through the window he could see the lighthouse rising above the trees. He was surprised at how near it was, like discovering how small a place you knew in childhood really is. He made coffee, grateful for its aroma, like a recovered loyalty. When he entered the sitting room in search of a cigarette, Lucrecia was watching him. She must have heard his footsteps along the passage and waited for him to appear in the doorway. She switched off the radio: the look in her eyes told him she had woken thinking he'd left. In the light of day she seemed less imperious, warmer, more fragile. She was suddenly grave, meek in the suspicion of danger, bracing herself against it.

'They've found Malcolm's body,' she said. 'They're looking for you.'

'Did they know my name?'

'Your full name and the hotel where you were staying. A ticket inspector said he saw you fighting on the train.'

'They must have found my coat,' said Biralbo. 'I was about to put it on when Malcolm appeared.'

'Did you leave your passport inside?'

Biralbo searched his pockets – he had his passport. Then he remembered.

'The hotel receipt,' he said. 'It was in my coat.'

'At least they don't have a photo of you.'

'Did they say I killed him?'

'No, just that they're looking for you. The ticket inspector remembered you and Malcolm very clearly. Apparently you were the only passengers on the train.'

'Have they identified Malcolm?'

'Even down to the profession on his passport. Picture restorer.'

'We've got to leave today, Lucrecia. Toussaints Morton will know where to find you.'

'Nobody will find us if we don't leave the house.'

'He knows the name of the station. He'll ask around. He'll find us in a couple of days.'

'But the airport police will have your name. You can't go back to your hotel and you can't leave Portugal.'

'I'll go by train.'

'They'll have police on the trains too.'

'I'll hide at Billy Swann's hotel for a few days.'

'Wait. I know someone who can help us. A Spaniard who has a club near the Burma. He'll get you some fake ID. He helped me with false papers for the painting.'

'Where does he live? I'll go and see him.'

'He can come here. I'll call him.'

'There's no time, Lucrecia. You have to get out of here.'

'We can leave together.'

'Call the man and tell him I'll go and see him. On my own.'

'You don't know anyone in Lisbon. You haven't got any money. In a few days' time we'll be able to leave safely.'

But he hardly felt the danger. Everything, even the thought that police cars might be patrolling the shady avenues of *quintas*, seemed far away and unconnected to him, as indifferent to his life as the view of the sea, the house and its neglected garden, and the distant passion of the previous night, free of the ash of the past, like the fire inside a diamond. He no longer needed to imprison time as he had in the past to keep Lucrecia close, to savour until the very last moment not only the pleasure but also the pain of having her near, like when he delayed playing the last few notes of a song from fear that silence would destroy the power of the music. Perhaps what he'd been given in the still light of dawn could not last or be commemorated or recovered: it would always be his so long as he didn't look back.

Without a word being spoken, Lucrecia knew what he was thinking and understood the tenderness of their silent parting. She kissed him lightly on the lips, then turned and went into the bedroom. Biralbo heard her dial and ask for someone in Portuguese. He brought her a cup of coffee and a cigarette. With a kind of clairvoyance, he knew that those gestures were part of their happiness. The phone wedged between her chin and her naked shoulder, Lucrecia spoke quickly with words he couldn't understand, and jotted something down in a notebook on her lap. She was wearing nothing but a large and slightly masculine shirt, with only a few buttons done up. Her hair was wet and a few drops of water still glistened on her thighs. She hung up, put the notebook and pencil on the bedside table and slowly drank her coffee, watching Biralbo.

'He's expecting you at four this afternoon,' she said, but her gaze was totally detached from her words. 'At this address.'

'Now call the airport.' Biralbo placed a cigarette between her lips and sat down beside her. 'Book a ticket on the first plane out of Portugal.'

Lucrecia folded the pillow and lay back against it, exhaling smoke through barely parted lips, in slow blue-grey wisps striped like shadow and light. She bent her knees and rested her bare feet on the edge of the bed.

'Are you sure you don't want to come with me?'

Biralbo stroked her heels – not a caress but a gentle acknowledgement. He parted her shirt a little and touched her still-damp skin. They looked at each other again. Their words and actions seemed as irrelevant to the intensity in their eyes as their cigarette smoke.

'Remember Morton, Lucrecia. He's the one we should be afraid of, not the police.'

'Is that the only reason?' Lucrecia took his cigarette from him and pulled him towards her, touching his lips and the wound on his forehead with her fingers.

'No, there's something else.'

'I thought so. What is it?'

'I'm playing with Billy Swann on the twelfth.'

'But it'll be dangerous. Someone might recognize you.'

'Not if I use a different name. I'll make sure the lights aren't on my face.'

'Don't play in Lisbon.' Lucrecia pushed him very gently so that he was lying beside her and took his face in her hands to make him look at her. 'Billy Swann will understand. It won't be his last concert.'

'It might be,' said Biralbo. He closed his eyes, and kissed the corners of her mouth, her cheeks, the roots of her hair, in a darkness more desirable than music and sweeter than oblivion.

'And you haven't seen her since?' I asked. 'You haven't even looked for her?'

'How was I going to look for her?' Biralbo glared at me. 'Where?'

'In Lisbon, I suppose, after a few months. The house was hers, wasn't it? She would have gone back there.'

'I phoned once. Nobody answered.'

'You should have written. Does she know you're living in Madrid?'

'I sent her a postcard a few days after I ran into you at the Metropolitano but it was sent back. "Address incomplete".'

'She must be looking for you.'

'Not for me, for Santiago Biralbo.' He searched for his passport in the bedside table and handed it to me, opened to the first page. 'She wouldn't be looking for Giacomo Dolphin.'

Short curly hair, dark glasses and several days' growth elongated the very pale, narrow face that now belonged to another
man – himself – who had spent many days holed up in a place that
wasn't exactly a hotel, waiting to look like the man in the photograph, because before taking it the Spaniard, Maraña, had
darkened his chin and cheeks with an eyeliner pencil and a small
brush smeared with grey powder. In front of the mirror, he'd
dabbed at Biralbo's face with damp fingers and greased back his
hair, as if doing the make-up for some second-rate actor, telling
him afterwards, satisfied with his work and carefully correcting
minor details while preparing the camera, 'Not even your mother
would recognize you now. Not even Lucrecia.'

For three days, shut up in a room with just one window from
which he could see a white dome, reddish roofs and a palm tree,
always waiting for Maraña to return with the fake passport, he
gradually transformed himself into that other, with the slowness of an invisible metamorphosis, as slowly as the beard grew
and soiled his face. Beneath the bare light bulb hanging from the
ceiling he smoked and looked out at the dome, and watched the
light outside turn from yellow to white and finally to blue-grey,
looking at himself in the mirror above the washbasin where a tap
dripped like a clock and gave off a smell of sewage when he
turned it on. He would rub his hands across his coarse cheeks, as
if searching for signs of a transfiguration not yet visible, and
count the hours and the drops of water, mumbling songs, imitating the sound of a trumpet or a double bass while from the
streets below the voices of Chinese girls called out to men and
laughed like birds, and the smell of barbecued meat and spicy
stews drifted up. As punctual as a nurse, one of those Chinese
girls, tiny and made up, with a disturbingly childlike politeness,

brought up coffee and plates of rice and fish, with white wine and brandy and smuggled American cigarettes, because Mr Maraña had ordered her to do so before he left. Once, she even lay down beside him and started to kiss him, like a bird pecking in the water, laughing afterwards with lowered eyes when Biralbo gently made her understand that he preferred to be alone. The Spaniard returned on the third day with the passport wrapped in a plastic bag, damp to the touch when Biralbo took it, because Maraña's hands and neck were always sweaty and he climbed the stairs from the street puffing like an elephant seal, wearing a colonial linen suit and glasses with green lenses that hid albino eyes, with his annoying, cunning hospitality. He ordered coffee and brandy and drove off the Chinese girls by clapping his hands. He kept his glasses on while he spoke to Biralbo, merely raising them slightly to wipe the lenses with the corner of a handkerchief.

'Giacomo Dolphin,' he said, bending the passport so that Biralbo would appreciate the quality of its flexibility. 'Born in Oran in nineteen fifty-one, of a Brazilian father, although he was born in Ireland, and an Italian mother. From today that's who you are, my friend. Have you seen the newspapers? They've stopped talking about that Yankee you took care of the other day. Neat work – a shame you left your coat on the train. Lucrecia explained everything to me. One push and on to the tracks, right?'

'I don't remember. In fact I'm not sure he didn't fall by himself.'

'Take it easy, man. We're compatriots, aren't we?' Maraña drank some brandy and sweat covered his face. 'I feel like a Spanish consul in Lisbon. They go to the embassy, or they come to me. As for that mulatto from Martinique who was looking for you, I already told Lucrecia: no need to worry. I'll take care of you personally until you leave Lisbon. I'll take you to the theatre where you're playing. In my own car. Is that mulatto armed?'

'I think so.'

'I do too.' Breathing heavily, Maraña extracted from his swollen waistband the largest revolver Biralbo had ever seen, even in the movies. 'Three fifty-seven. Just let him get in front of me.'

'He tends to come up from behind. With a nylon cord.'

'Well he better not let me turn around.' Maraña got to his feet and put the revolver away. 'I've got to go. Can I take you anywhere?'

'The theatre, if you can. I have a rehearsal.'

'At your service. For Lucrecia I'm willing to be a passport forger, bodyguard and taxi driver. I do you a favour today, you do me one tomorrow. That's the business world: today for you, tomorrow for me. Oh, and if you need money, just ask. You're lucky, my friend. This living off women . . .'

Maraña came to pick him up every evening, wedged into an implausible car that climbed through the tiny streets like a cockroach, one of those Morrises that were very sporty twenty years ago; Biralbo always wondered how Maraña could get into it and manoeuvre. While he drove, almost squashed to the roof, he snorted through the sea-lion moustache which covered his mouth, manhandling the wheel with brusque and arbitrary turns. Sometimes he was a political refugee from the old days, at others a fugitive from an unjust charge of embezzlement. He no longer felt any nostalgia for Spain, that land of ingratitude and envy that condemned to exile those who rebelled against its mediocrity; wasn't Biralbo also an exile? Hadn't he had to travel to foreign lands to triumph with his music? During rehearsals Maraña sat in the front row smiling, like a wax Buddha, or dozing peacefully, and when a drum-roll or an eruption of silence woke him he reached quickly for his revolver and examined the shadows of the empty theatre with its half-drawn red curtains. Biralbo never dared ask how much Lucrecia had paid Maraña or what debt he was discharging by protecting him. 'In exile, we Spaniards have to help one another,' he would say, 'just like the Jews . . .'

But on the evening of the concert Biralbo didn't wait to hear the car's horn or the catastrophic noise it made when it rode over the paving-stones and stopped at the door, beside the window where the Chinese girls sometimes perched. He got off the bed like an invalid driven by the obligation of courage, drank a shot of brandy and looked at himself in the mirror: his dilated pupils and eight-day beard gave him the air of a sordid life and sleepless nights. He put away his passport like it was a weapon, put on dark glasses and went down the narrow staircase that was covered with a filthy oil-cloth. One of the girls said goodbye to him from the window. He heard short, sharp laughter behind him, but didn't turn round. Smoke thick with the smell of grease and resin and oriental food emerged from a nearby tavern. His dark glasses made the world seem opaque, like night or an eclipse. As he descended towards the lower town he felt the same almost involuntary lightness as when about halfway through a set he lost his fear of the music, and his hands stopped sweating and obeyed an instinct for speed and pride as removed from conscious thought as the beating of his heart. Turning a corner, he saw the whole city and the bay, with ships in the distance and cranes at the port, and the bridge hazy and red over the water shrouded in opalescent mist. Only his instinct for music guided him and kept him from becoming lost, leading him to places he recognized from his search for Lucrecia, pushing him past damp passageways and walled-up alleys, towards Lisbon's vast squares and statue-topped columns, arriving at the slightly seedy theatre, where the syncopated lights and shadows of the earliest films shone, relics from the end of another century only found in Lisbon. He told me that the façade of the theatre bore a sign decorated with nymphs and allegorical figures and sinuous letters forming the strange word 'Animatograph', and that even before reaching the wide, identical streets of the lower city he began to see the posters on which his new name was written below Billy Swann's in big red characters, GIACOMO DOLPHIN, PIANO.

He saw yellow houses perched on the hills, one on top of the other, and the cold December sun, and the stairway and slender metal lift tower that one evening in the distant past had temporarily saved him from Malcolm; he saw the dark doorways of the warehouses and the windows of office buildings already lit, the murmuring crowd that gathered beneath blue neon signs as night fell, as if waiting for or witnessing something – perhaps the invisibility or secret destiny of the man with dark glasses and furtive gestures no longer called Santiago Biralbo, who had been born out of nothingness in Lisbon.

When he arrived at the theatre people were already hanging around the ticket office; he told me that in Lisbon there are always people everywhere, even in public urinals and entrances to pornographic cinemas, in the places that seem most severely condemned to solitude, on street corners near stations, always men on their own, in dark clothes, badly shaven, as if they'd just got off an overnight express train, coppery-skinned white men with sidelong glances, silent black and Asian men who endure their destinies with infinite melancholy, as exiles in a city on the other side of the world. But there, at the entrance to the Animatograph, he saw the same pale faces he'd seen in northern Europe, the same gestures of cultured patience and resourcefulness, and thought that neither he nor Billy Swann had ever played for those people because, although they were there and would quietly buy their tickets, the music they were about to hear would never move them.

But this was something Billy Swann had always known, and maybe it didn't bother him, because whenever he walked out to play it was as if he was alone, defended and isolated by the spotlights that plunged the audience into darkness and marked an irrevocable boundary at the edge of the stage. Billy Swann was in his dressing room, indifferent to the lights around the mirror and the damp, dirty walls, a cigarette between his lips, his trumpet on his knees, a bottle of fruit juice within reach, alien, aloof and alone, docile as if in a doctor's waiting room. He seemed not to recognize Biralbo or anybody else, not even Oscar, who brought him suspicious-looking pills and glasses of water and made sure nobody broke the circle of solitude and silence that surrounded him.

'I'm here, Billy,' said Biralbo.

'I'm not.' Billy Swann lifted his cigarette to his mouth again, but strangely, with a rigid hand, like someone only pretending to smoke. His voice was slower and more sombre and less intelligible than ever. 'What can you see with those glasses on?'

'Practically nothing.' Biralbo took them off. The light from the bare bulb hurt his eyes and the dressing room seemed smaller. 'Maraña told me to wear them all the time.'

'I see everything in black and white.' Billy Swann was talking to the wall. 'Or in grey and grey. Darker or lighter. Not like in films. The way insects see things. I read a book about it. They don't see colours. When I was young I could see colours. When I smoked grass I could see a green light around everything. With whisky it was different: more yellow and more red, more blue, like when the spotlights come on.'

'I've told them not to point them at your face,' said Oscar.

'Is she coming tonight?' Billy Swann turned slowly and wearily towards Biralbo, the same way he was talking: there was a story in each word he uttered.

'She's gone,' said Biralbo.

'Where?' Billy Swann sipped his juice with disgust and obedience.

'I don't know,' said Biralbo. 'I told her to go.'

'She'll come back.' Billy Swann held out his hand and Biralbo helped him up. He seemed to weigh nothing.

'Nine o'clock,' said Oscar. 'Time to go on.' Very close by, behind the stage, they could hear the sound of the audience. It scared Biralbo as much as hearing the sea in the darkness.

'I've been earning my living like this for forty years.' Billy Swann walked leaning on Biralbo's arm, clutching his trumpet against his chest as if he were afraid to lose it. 'And I still can't understand why they come to hear us or why we play for them.'

'We don't play for them, Billy,' said Oscar. The four of them, with the blond French drummer, Buby, gathered at the end of a line of curtains, the stage-lights already illuminating their faces.

Biralbo's mouth felt dry and his palms were sweating. From the other side of the curtains he could hear voices and scattered whistling. 'In those theatres it's like walking out into a circus,' he once told me. 'It's a relief if someone else goes on first, to be devoured by the lions.' Buby went on first, head down, smiling, moving with the quick stealth of a nocturnal animal, rhythmically tapping the sides of his jeans. There was brief applause; Oscar appeared behind him, fat and wavering, with an impassive attitude of disdain. The double bass and drums were already playing when Biralbo came out on stage. The lights blinded him, bright yellow fires passing through the lenses of his glasses, but he saw only the striped white length of the keyboard. Placing his hands on it was like grabbing on to the last plank of a shipwreck. Clumsy and afraid, he began an old song, looking at his tense white hands that moved as if they wanted to escape. Buby made the drums roll with the violence of high walls tumbling down, and then brushed circles on the cymbals, imposing silence. Biralbo watched Billy Swann walk past him and stop at the edge of the stage, barely lifting his feet from the platform as though moving blindly or afraid to wake somebody up.

He raised his trumpet and put the mouthpiece to his lips. He closed his eyes, his face tense and reddened, but still didn't start to play. He seemed to be bracing himself for a blow. His back to the band, he made a sign with his hand, as if trying to stroke an animal. A sudden feeling of imminence shook Biralbo. He looked at Oscar, leaning forward with his eyes closed, his left hand resting on the neck of the bass, avidly expectant and wise. It seemed to him then that he was listening to the whisper of an impossible voice, that he saw once again the captivating landscape of the violet mountain and the path and house hidden among the trees. That night, he told me, Billy Swann wasn't even playing for them, his witnesses and accomplices. He was playing for himself, for the darkness and silence, for the sombre, faceless heads that swayed almost imperceptibly beyond the curtain of light, anonymous eyes and ears and beating hearts, profiles lined up along a calm abyss into which Billy Swann alone, armed with his trumpet – not even his trumpet, which he handled as if it didn't exist – dared look. Biralbo wanted to follow him, leading the others, to advance to meet he who was alone and far away and turned away, to envelop him in a warm and powerful current, and for a moment Billy Swann seemed to acquiesce as if held there by fatigue, but then fled as from a lie or resignation, because maybe what they were playing was a lie and cowardly. Like an animal that knows its pursuers can't catch it, he would suddenly change the direction of his flight, or stay absolutely still, sniffing the air, establishing with his music an inaudible perimeter that surrounded him like a glass bell, creating his own beat within the drilled tempo of the others.

When Biralbo looked up from the piano he could see Billy Swann's profile, flushed and tense, his eyelids squeezed tight like double scars. Unable to follow him, they were dispersing, each of the three floundering in his pursuit; only Oscar plucked the strings of the bass with tenacity, alien to any rhythm, without giving in to Billy Swann's silence and distance. After a few minutes Oscar's hands stopped moving too. Billy Swann lowered his trumpet from his mouth and Biralbo thought several hours must have passed, that the concert must be about to end, but nobody applauded, there wasn't a sound in the overawed darkness where the last sharp note of the trumpet still hung. So close to the microphone that his breathing sounded like a deep rumble, Billy Swann was singing. I know how he sang, I've heard him on records, but Biralbo told me I'll never be able to imagine the sound of his voice that night: it was a murmur, dispossessed of music, a slow chant, a strange oration, harsh and tender, savage and profound and muffled, as though to hear it you had to put your ear to the ground. Raising his hands, caressing the keyboard as though searching for a crack in the silence, Biralbo began to play, guided and accepted by the voice like a blind man, imagining suddenly that Lucrecia was listening in the shadows, judging him, but even that didn't matter: all he cared about was the quiet hypnotic voice finally showing him his destiny and the single and serene justification of his life, the explanation of everything, of things he'd never understand, the futility of fear and the right to pride, of the dark certainty of something that was neither suffering nor happiness and yet contained both indecipherably, as well as his old love for Lucrecia and his three years of solitude and their mutual recognition at dawn in the house on the cliffs. Now he saw it all in a calm and elated light like a cold winter morning along a street in Lisbon or San Sebastian. As if waking up he realized that he could no longer hear Billy Swann's voice – he was playing alone, and Oscar and the drummer were staring at him. Beside the piano, facing him, Billy Swann was wiping his glasses, slowly tapping his foot and moving his head, as if approving something he could hear in the distance.

'Did he ever drink again?'

'Not a drop.' Biralbo got up off the bed and went to open the balcony window; there was now a gleam of sun on the roofs of the buildings, on the highest windows of the Telefónica building. He turned and showed me the empty bottle. 'But he didn't give up alcohol, or music. They simply came to an end in Lisbon. Like this bottle. That's why he didn't care if he was alive or dead.'

He opened the curtains and threw the empty bottle in the bin. It seemed as if in the light of the morning we no longer knew each other. I looked at him, thinking I should leave, but not knowing what to say. I've never known how to say goodbye.

I spent the next few days in a town not far from Madrid. When I returned I thought it was finally time to write to Floro Bloom – I'd heard nothing from him since I left San Sebastian. I didn't have his address so I decided to ask Biralbo. I called at his hotel and was told he wasn't there. For some reason I can't now recall it took a few days for me to go to see him at the Metropolitano. Returning to places I had been ten or twenty years ago doesn't affect me, but if I go back to a bar where I've been a regular only a fortnight or a month later, I feel an intolerable hollowness in the time which has passed over things in my absence and submitted them to invisible changes without my knowledge, like leaving your house for a while with untrustworthy tenants.

The poster for the Giacomo Dolphin Trio was no longer on the door of the Metropolitano. It was still early; a waiter I didn't know

told me that Monica's shift started at eight. I didn't ask for Biralbo
and his band – I remembered it was the day they didn't play there.
I ordered a beer and drank it slowly at a table at the back. Monica
arrived a few minutes before eight. She didn't see me at first, she
only looked round when the waiter said something to her. Her hair
was a mess and she'd put on her make-up in a hurry. But then she
always seemed to arrive at the last possible moment. Without
taking off her coat she sat down opposite me: by the way she
looked at me I could tell she was going to ask about Biralbo. From
her mouth it didn't sound strange to hear him called Giacomo.

'He disappeared ten days ago,' she said. We'd never spoken
alone. I noticed for the first time that there were hints of violet in
her eyes. 'Without saying a word to me. But Buby and Oscar knew
he was about to go. They've gone too.'

'Did he leave alone?'

'I thought you'd know.' She looked straight at me and the colour
of her eyes became more intense. She didn't trust me.

'He never told me his plans.'

'He never seemed to have any.' Monica smiled stiffly, the way
someone smiles when lost. 'Is it true he was sick?'

I told her it was, weaving together some half-truths she pretended to accept, inventing some details that were more or less
false, not exactly benign, perhaps useless, like those told to a
patient whose pain isn't important to us. Finally she asked, suspicious and disdainful, if there was another woman. I said no, trying
to look her in the eye, assured her that I was going to keep searching, that I would return, and wrote my home telephone number on
a napkin which she put in her bag. Later, when I said goodbye, I
realized without sadness that she wasn't looking at me.

It had started to drizzle when I left the Metropolitano. Looking up at the large fluorescent letters I tried to imagine how the night would be at exactly that second in Lisbon; I thought perhaps Biralbo had returned there. I walked to his hotel. On the other side of the street, under the windows of the Telefónica building, you could already see the women gathering, cigarettes between their lips, wearing large overcoats with the collars turned up to their chins because an icy wind blew along the darkened footpaths. Above the hotel awning, next to the vertical sign, still unlit, I made out Biralbo's window. It was dark. I crossed the street and stood outside the hotel entrance. Two men, very much alike in black jackets and sunglasses and identical moustaches, were talking to the receptionist. I didn't step forward to open the automatic doors. The receptionist stared at me, still explaining something to the two men, his neutral gaze moving from me to study the glass doors indifferently, and returning to the two men. He was showing them the hotel register, and as he turned the pages he glanced at the badge one of them had put down on the desk. I went in and pretended to read the list of room prices. From behind the two men looked identical; the receptionist looked at me again, but nobody else would have noticed. Putting his badge in the back pocket of his jeans, from which shone the edge of a pair of handcuffs, I heard one of them say, 'Please let us know if he comes back.'

The receptionist slammed shut the wide pages of the register. The two men in jackets made an excessive show of shaking his hand. Then they went out into the street: the car parked at an angle outside the hotel started up before they got in. I was smoking and pretending to wait for the lift. The receptionist called my name, gesturing towards the door with relief. 'They've finally gone,' he said, handing me a key that he didn't take from the pigeonholes. 307. Apologetically he explained that Toussaints Morton – 'the coloured guy' – and the blonde woman who accompanied him had searched Mr Dolphin's room, but by the time he called the police it was already too late: they had left by the fire escape.

'If they'd arrived ten minutes earlier they'd have found him,' he said. 'Their lifts must have passed each other.'

'But hadn't Mr Dolphin left?'

'He didn't come in all week.' The receptionist took a certain pride in displaying complicity with Biralbo. 'But I kept his room for him, he didn't even take his luggage. He came back this afternoon in a terrible hurry. He told me before he went up to order him a taxi.'

'You don't know where he was going?'

'Not far. He only took one bag. He said that if you came I was to give you the key to his room.'

'Did he say anything else?'

'You know Mr Dolphin.' The receptionist smiled. 'A man of few words.'

I went up to the room. The receptionist had given me the key merely as a gesture of courtesy – the lock was broken. The bed was unmade and the drawers were turned over on the floor. There was a smell in the air like damp logs burning, a delicate and precise odour that took me back to the night in San Sebastian when I first saw Daphne. On the carpet, among the clothes and papers, a cigar butt had burnt a dark circle like a stain. I found a black and white photo of Lucrecia, a book in English about Billy Swann, some dog-eared sheet music, a few cheap thrillers, an unopened bottle of bourbon.

I opened the window. The drizzle and cold struck me in the face. I closed the shutters and the curtains, and lit a cigarette. On the shelf in the bathroom I found a perspex cup so opaque it looked dirty. I tried to forget that it had the squalor of glasses people use for soaking their false teeth, and filled it with bourbon. Obeying an old superstition, I filled it again before it was empty. I could hear the muffled sound of traffic, of the lift that sometimes stopped close by, steps and voices in the hotel hallways. I drank slowly, without conviction or aim, the same way one stares at a street in a strange city. I sat on the bed, the cup between my knees. The bottle of bourbon glowed red in the light of the bedside lamp. I'd drunk about half of it when I heard cautious knocking at the door. I didn't move: if someone came in, I'd have my back to them, but I wasn't going to turn round. They knocked again, three taps, like an agreed signal. Dulled and sluggish with the bourbon, I went to the door, without realizing I was still holding the bottle. It was the first thing Lucrecia looked at, not my face, which maybe she didn't recognize until a little later, when she said my name.

The alcohol limited my surprise at seeing her. She was no longer as I had known her or even as I had imagined her from Biralbo's words. She seemed very alone, with the urgency of someone who has just got off a train. She was wearing an open white raincoat, which was wet, and the cold and damp from outside followed her in. Before entering the empty room she looked at the disarray and the bottle I was holding. I told her to come in. Out of an absurd sense of hospitality, I raised the bottle a bit and offered her a drink. There was nowhere for her to sit. Standing in the middle of the room, facing me, without removing her hands from the pockets of her raincoat, she asked me about Biralbo. As if apologizing for his absence, I told her that he had left, that I was there to pick up his things. She nodded, looking again at the open drawers, the dim lamp. In its light, and because of the aimless fervour of the bourbon, Lucrecia's face had the perfection and distance of a woman in a glossy magazine. She seemed taller and more alone than women in real life and her gaze was different.

'You should leave too,' I said. 'Toussaints Morton has been here.'

'Don't you know where Santiago's gone?'

It seemed to me that name didn't refer to Biralbo; I had never heard anyone call him that, not even Floro Bloom.

'The rest of his band's left too,' I said. I felt that a single word would be enough to keep Lucrecia there for a moment, but I didn't know what it was. Without saying anything more, she turned around and I heard the brush of her raincoat through the air, then the slow noise of the lift.

I closed the door and poured some more bourbon into my glass. From the balcony windows I saw her appear on the pavement, her back towards me, slightly bent over, the white raincoat flowing in the cold December wind, glistening in the rain under the blue lights of the hotel. I recognized her way of walking as she crossed the street, now a distant white smudge in the crowd, lost in it, invisible, suddenly erased behind the open umbrellas and cars, as if she had never existed.